LJ BURKHART

Light Me Up

A Fire Novel

First edition

This book was professionally typeset on Reedsy.
Find out more at reedsy.com

Contents

Chapter 1

Lauren

The first thing I noticed was that there was a constant beeping near me. It was extremely aggravating. It was almost immediately after that I realized what a horrible headache I had. I couldn't focus on anything but the pain and the annoying noise. Until I heard someone say my name.

"Lauren? Can you hear me?" I didn't recognize whoever was talking to me. It was a woman, her high-pitched voice making my headache even worse.

I slowly tried opening my eyes, but quickly closed them, groaning in pain when my head exploded. I tried again, slower this time, and found myself staring up at a middle-aged nurse, who was kindly staring back at me. I looked around the room; it seemed that I was in the hospital. That should have been evident from the moment I heard the beeping, but my thoughts were extremely foggy.

"Good morning, honey. How are you feeling?" the nurse asked me, sympathy and concern staining her features.

"I have an awful headache, and it hurts to breathe," I said, my throat raw and scratchy. The nurse, seeming to read my mind, grabbed a glass of water and held the straw up to my mouth. I sipped gratefully, draining half. "What happened?"

"Ummm, let me go get someone to talk to you, sweetie. Hang tight, I'll be right back," she said, scurrying away, looking uncomfortable.

I had a sinking feeling. Something was very wrong. I clutched my stomach, praying to whatever god was listening that my baby was okay. I didn't remember what happened, or why I was here. The last thing I could remember was sitting on the couch with Ryan watching *Outlander*, but I had a feeling that a lot had happened between then and now.

A moment later, a doctor and a police officer walked in the room, and my dread and anxiety multiplied by ten.

"How are you feeling, Lauren?" the doctor asked me.

"Just tell me what's going on," I said, my panic getting the better of me.

"Ma'am, you were in a car accident." The police officer finally spoke.

"I don't even remember being in a car. Was anyone with me? Is my baby okay?"

The two men exchanged glances before looking back at me with sympathy and regret written all over their faces. The doctor spoke first.

"Well, you've sustained some injuries. You have a concussion and some broken ribs."

"What about my baby?!" I practically screamed at him.

"I'm so sorry, Lauren. Since you weren't yet in your second trimester, the fetus couldn't handle the trauma. You had a miscarriage."

My hands drifted to my stomach, clutching at my now-empty womb. I felt tears streaming down my face as I sobbed uncontrollably. My ribs were screaming in pain, but it was nothing compared to the feeling of my heart breaking. I needed Ryan. He was the only one who could get me through this.

"Where's my fiancé? Where's Ryan?" I asked through my sobs.

"Ryan was the one driving, ma'am. Your car was T-boned by a drunk driver who fled the scene. Ryan's side was the one that was hit. I'm so sorry, ma'am, but he was killed on impact," the police officer said, ending my entire world.

I had lost all concept of time. I sat in the hospital bed, going in between sleep and an all-consuming depression whenever I woke to realize that it was not in fact a terrible dream. I didn't interact with any of the staff. I didn't even hear them when they tried talking to me. Nothing felt real. My whole world had crumbled, and being here in this hospital room without anyone I knew, I felt completely lost.

One of the nurses brought a tray of food and set it down in front of me. I realized absently that it was the nurse from when I first woke up.

"Miss, you really need to eat," she told me, finally breaking through my bubble. White-hot rage broke through it right at the same moment.

I picked up the tray and hurled it at the wall, startling the nurse in front of me. "I don't want to eat! I want to die and be with my baby and my fiancé!" I screamed at her. Just then, I heard Savannah's voice calling my name from the doorway.

"Lauren, honey." I looked up to see Savannah and Anna in the doorway, white lilies in Savannah's hands and "Get Well Soon!" balloons in Anna's, sorrow and concern etching their features. As soon as I saw them, I broke down into sobs once again.

Savannah quickly made her way across the room, got up on the bed, and crushed me to her chest. "Lauren, I'm so sorry," she said, her voice cracking.

"Ryan and my baby" was all I could get out through the sobs overtaking me.

"Shh. I know," Savannah said, rocking me back and forth. Anna's hand was on my back. I fell asleep cradled there with my friends supporting me.

Chapter 2

Phoenix

Charlie and I were eating dinner at the firehouse, shooting the shit, when we got a call about a car accident. We quickly got into our truck and drove over. The scene of the wreck was an absolute shit show. As we finally made our way through the traffic and debris, there appeared to be only one car there, and by the looks of it, the other car had to be barely functioning. I was surprised they were able to drive away at all. Careless motherfuckers. They were probably drunk, I thought as I rolled my eyes and got out of the truck.

The driver's-side door was completely smashed in, indicating the car had been T-boned. My team was already getting the jaws of life ready to get the driver out. I made my way over to the passenger side, with Charlie right behind me. Witnesses already had the door open, but weren't touching whoever it was, which was smart. Too many people died or became paralyzed because people moved them when they had a neck or back injury. Obviously if the person wasn't breathing it was a different story, and I assumed this person was, otherwise they would be doing CPR.

As soon as the passenger came into view, I recognized the silvery-purple hair immediately, and I prayed that I was wrong about who it was. I ran faster and moved everyone out of the way as I approached. Sure enough, it was Lauren. She had blood on her forehead and she was unconscious. Charlie came up behind me, and swore under his breath upon seeing her. We both worked quickly getting her out of the car and onto the gurney that the EMTs brought upon getting there. They checked her vitals and reported that she was physically fine, besides some minor injuries. As soon as they started wheeling her away, I noticed the massive amount of blood in between her legs, and my heart broke for her. I didn't even think, I just ran to her and jumped in the ambulance with the paramedics.

"Charlie, I'm riding with her. I don't want her to be alone. Call the girls and meet me at the hospital," I told him, hating the thought of leaving her by herself in case she woke up in the ambulance.

A strange look crossed his face, but he nodded and took out his cell, no doubt calling Savannah.

The ambulance drove away, and I looked down at the woman on the gurney. I couldn't explain it, but I was drawn to her from the second I met her. Of course as soon as I realized that she was engaged, I backed off, not wanting to cause any trouble, but I thought about how unlucky I was, that I had finally found a woman I could see myself with, and she was happy with another man and a baby on the way. Now, I felt so guilty for thinking any such thing. She had probably lost her baby, and from the looks of that car, her future husband too.

I hated to think of the pain she would be in when she woke up to find out her entire world had come crashing down around her. For some unknown reason, I felt this intense need to protect her. I would turn back time for her if I could, just so she could have Ryan and her baby back.

I held her hand as the EMTs checked her vitals again, telling me that she had lost some blood, but other than that, her numbers looked good.

I was able to breathe a sigh of relief after that news, but still didn't let go of her hand. Just before we reached the hospital, she started stirring. Her eyes opened, and she looked at me but didn't really see me.

"Ryan, are we going to have our baby? Is that why we're in an ambulance?" she asked me with love and excitement in her gaze, clearly hallucinating, no doubt from the pain from her probable miscarriage. I couldn't break her heart yet, not when she wasn't lucid. I might be going to hell for this, but it was all I could do.

"Yes, baby. Now just relax and get some rest," I said soothingly, trying to coax her back to sleep so the doctors could work once we arrived.

"Okay, honey. I can't wait to meet our little one," she said, pulling my head down to kiss me before passing out again.

Guilt and sorrow threatened to pull me under, but I pushed through it. I took comfort that when she woke up, she wouldn't remember any of this.

But I would. And as much as I hated myself for it, my heart skipped a beat with that kiss.

Chapter 3

Lauren

Three months later...

I was still in the same spot I was when the accident happened. Severely depressed. Extremely angry. Constantly anxious. The only time I left my apartment was to go to work, but even then, my tips were absolute shit because I was a complete and utter bitch to everyone who was unlucky enough to sit in my chair. I was sure Floyd's Barbershop was tempted to fire me because of all of my customer complaints, but they were reluctant to do so because of what had happened.

My life had become stagnant. Everything was the same as it was before, except for what I had lost. I was still in the same small, shitty, overpriced apartment that I lived in before Ryan passed. I hated it here, but couldn't force myself to leave. It felt like the only remaining connection that I had with him. Not to mention that I could never afford to live on my own anywhere else in this goddamn city.

I was also still at the same shitty job as before. I still hadn't figured out what I wanted to do as a career, and it was slowly driving me mad.

One of the only things that I did change was my hair. I had my original hair color for the first time since I was thirteen years old.

I no longer felt like the vibrant, eccentric, life-loving woman that I used to be. My personality now matched my dirty dishwater blonde: depressing and plain. At least it was on me. I thought it looked pretty on others, but on me, who had every hair color under the sun, I just looked sunken and washed out, exactly what I was aiming for.

I knew everyone was very concerned for my well-being, but I couldn't bring myself to care. My family had come to visit me right after it happened. My dad and my sister came for about a week, and my mom came with them, but stayed for about a month. After she left, my best friend, Jessa, visited for a little over a week, not able to stay longer because of work.

I appreciated all of them coming, and I even had a little fun, but I don't think they understood that I wasn't the same person anymore. I didn't think I would ever be that woman again.

All of them tried to convince me to move back to Michigan with them, and I thought about it, but I realized that I would just be going backward. As much as going forward without Ryan hurt, going backward would hurt just as bad, because he still wouldn't be there. And there would be a million more memories of him there as well.

I had the day off work, and I had spent the entirety of it sitting on the couch watching horror films. I couldn't watch anything with any sort of romance in it, otherwise I would either get super pissed and throw something at the TV, or I would break down into painful sobs for hours.

The only thing that kept me going was the thought of finding the son of the bitch who did this to me. I wanted them fucking dead. They ripped my world to shreds and then they disappeared, leaving my fiancé and baby dead. If I ever found them, they were going to wish they were dead before I was finished.

At five o'clock, I heard a knock on the door. Fully intending to ignore whoever was on the other side, I sank deeper into the couch cushions and turned the volume up. The knocking continued for two minutes and when I finally turned the volume down to a normal level, I heard Anna yelling.

"Open up, bitch! I will break this damn door down!"

I rolled my eyes as I unlocked the door, intending to tell her to fuck off, when she barreled in, obviously figuring out my plan, since I did that to her the last time she showed up.

"Bitch, please. You need to learn some new tricks," she told me with a twinkle in her eye.

"Yeah, well, I haven't had the time to learn anything new," I said sarcastically.

"Oh yeah? And what, may I ask, has been taking up so much of your time?"

"Wallowing in self-pity really takes up a big chunk of the day, you know," I joked, smiling despite myself.

Anna chuckled and leaned in for a long hug. I broke away before I started to get emotional. Lately, I couldn't stand anyone touching me for very long.

"Okay, so I brought a box of wine. Savannah will be here in a half hour when she gets off work, and we are going to get absolutely shit-faced. And I see your face and know that you are about to tell me no, but I don't care. I know you have tomorrow off, so you have no excuse."

I sighed, knowing that there was no way I could convince her to leave.

"Okay, fine. But we do not watch anything romantic or I will literally kick you bitches out on your asses," I relented.

"Deal," she said, smiling triumphantly.

We were already a glass of wine in when Savannah showed up. She quickly caught up to us and we settled into our normal rhythm and banter. As much as I didn't want to admit it, it felt really nice having them here. Everything felt normal, even if just for a little while.

Then the guilt crept in. How could I be enjoying myself when Ryan wasn't here with me? I felt tears start to stream silently down my face. The girls didn't notice at first because they were arguing over who was hotter, Charlie Hunnam or Sam Heughan.

"Oh, honey, what's wrong?" Savannah asked, pulling me in for a hug.

"I shouldn't be having fun. I shouldn't be enjoying myself without him," I sobbed into her shoulder. They let me cry for a few minutes before Savannah pulled back.

"Lauren, you need to listen to us. You have done nothing wrong. I know you're still having such a hard time, which is totally understandable, but you're allowed to have fun and enjoy yourself too," Anna said.

"Yes, how do you think Ryan would feel if he saw you like this? He would want you to be happy, and to eventually move on. He wouldn't want you to be alone and miserable forever." Savannah added, "Would you want him to be miserable if the roles were reversed?"

"No, but don't talk about me being with anyone else, okay? I'm definitely not there yet," I said, not able to give them any other answer.

"Okay, babe. Just don't shut yourself off to it forever, okay?" Savannah said.

"Yeah, 'cause otherwise we will intervene, and trust me, you don't want me to intervene," Anna added. I laughed, appreciating the comic relief.

"Okay, bitches, let's move on to something a little more pleasant. Let's make some shitty food and some brownies, huh?" Savannah insisted.

"Ooh yes! I brought Totino's pizzas for all of us. I call the pepperoni, so you ladies can duke it out between the cheese and the combination pizzas," Anna said.

We all went into the kitchen and spent the next half hour making food and laughing, smearing the brownie batter onto each other's faces, and eating half of the batter before putting it in the oven.

11

"Hey, so I actually have something for you both. I've been wanting to give them to you for a while, but it's been a minute since we were all together," Savannah said a half hour later when we were all hanging out in the living room. She reached into her bag and got out two bottles of wine.

"More wine? We've already had plenty, in case you didn't notice," Anna remarked sarcastically.

Savannah rolled her eyes and flipped her off before handing them over to us. The front of the bottles had a picture of the three of us on it, with the words "Will you bitches be my Maids of Honor?

"Oh, hell yes," Anna exclaimed, wrapping Savannah in a quick hug, beaming.

"Uh, Savannah, are you sure you want me?" I asked, unsure.

"Of course! Why wouldn't I want you in my wedding?"

"I've just been such a downer with everything going on lately, and I understand if you don't want me to be part of your happy occasion since I'm so pissy," I said.

"Bitch, please. I can handle all your surliness and more. I'll be upset if you tell me you aren't going to be in my wedding," she said jokingly, putting me at ease.

"Okay, if you're sure, just as long as Anna walks first," I said.

"Deal."

It was a fantastic night, and I hadn't been this happy since Ryan passed. I finally felt a tiny sliver of my old self slide back into place.

The next morning, I woke up to the girls cuddling with me. After finishing off the box of wine the night before, we turned on *Young Frankenstein* in the bedroom and all squished into my queen-size bed before falling into a deep sleep. I tried carefully extracting myself from them to use the bathroom, but had no such luck.

"Shit, what time is it?" Savannah asked, bolting straight up in bed.

"It's just after nine, bitch, now quiet down so I can go back to sleep," Anna grumbled next to me.

"Crap. I have to be at work by ten," Savannah said, scrambling out of bed.

"Don't you dare use the toilet before me!" I yelled, racing after her.

She turned on the shower while I took care of business. Savannah started undressing in front of me and got in the shower, rushing so that she wouldn't be late. I always thought it was so funny how different men and women were. Men would never be this comfortable in front of each other. It was one of the things I loved about having best friends. We were always open with each other and were just ourselves with no judgments.

"Why are you even taking a shower if you're in such a hurry?" Anna asked crankily. "And don't turn it off 'cause I want to take one too," she said as she too started undressing, making me chuckle to myself.

"I need to take one 'cause I reek of booze!" Savannah yelled. "And I think I still have brownie batter all over me." She quickly got out of the shower as Anna stepped in. I held out a towel for her and sat on the toilet seat, just enjoying waking up with people and feeling somewhat normal again.

Savannah, like always, could never be without music, so she grabbed her phone and turned on Bishop Briggs before she started doing her makeup in her towel.

I decided to see if I had anything to make for breakfast while the girls were getting ready. All I had in the fridge was one egg, so that wouldn't be enough. When I dug through the pantry I came across a box of Belgian waffle mix and some syrup. Perfect, I thought. I just needed to add an egg and some oil.

Fifteen minutes later, I had the waffles finished and coffee made. The girls both came out at the same time, Savannah ready for the day, and Anna with a towel around her head and my robe on.

"Hey, I never said you could use my robe."

"Yeah, but I knew you would've said yes, so I put it on anyway," she said, shrugging and sitting down. She grabbed one of the waffles before topping it with a bunch of peanut butter and syrup.

"Well, you don't know me very well, because I would've told you that I didn't want your dirty cooch getting my robe all nasty," I joked with her.

"Hey, cunt, I'll have you know, I just took a shower, so it isn't dirty… anymore," Anna replied, making us all laugh.

After we were finished eating, Savannah kissed us both on the mouth before taking off for work. Anna had the day off like me, so she stuck around for a while. We hung out on the couch and watched *Inside Out* and laughed our asses off. I absolutely loved animated movies. Especially when it was Disney or Pixar. They made me feel comfortable, like I was home after being away for a long time.

We finished the movie and Anna convinced me to go to lunch with her, even though I really didn't want to be out in public. We decided to get Indian food, which I hadn't had in a long time. After we were seated and had our drinks in front of us, we got in line for the buffet. I mainly just loaded up on rice and chicken tikka masala. It was my absolute favorite and I could never get enough. Then, of course, after we finished our meals, we went back for the carrot pudding. Anna had convinced me to try it, and I was hooked. It was one of the most delicious desserts I had ever had.

As we were sitting there, eating way too much, Anna looked at me, took a drink of her beer, and then sighed.

"Lauren, I'm worried about you," she said. "There's something that I want to talk to you about. Before you say no, just please think about it."

"Ooookay," I said skeptically.

"I think you should move in with me," she blurted out. "I know that you hate that apartment, and that without Ryan's income, you're struggling. I've been looking for a roommate for a while now, but I haven't found anyone. Plus, I would like to live with someone who I already trust, and we just have so much fun together. I really don't like you living alone with everything going on. You just shut everyone out, and you clearly need to be with people as opposed to stuck in your own head," she spouted quickly, as if scared that I wouldn't let her finish her little speech.

I sat there quietly for a moment, contemplating everything that she had said. I did hate my apartment, and I didn't think it was healthy for me to still live there. She was right. It wasn't doing me any good to continue on the way I had been. I needed to make at least one change, and this one would make my life easier.

"Okay. I'll move in."

Chapter 4

Lauren

One year later...

I walked into the apartment that I shared with Anna, tired after a long day of work. Immediately upon entering, I went to the kitchen and poured myself a huge glass of wine and took a long drink. My next stop was my bedroom to change out of my hair-infested clothes. I was always so itchy after cutting hair all day.

Once I was in comfy clothes, I headed into the living room where I plopped myself down on the sofa. I sighed as I took in my surroundings. I loved this apartment. It was kind of a mix between boho, industrial, and punk. There was so much exposed brick all around and sliding barn doors. There was also a spiral staircase in the kitchen that led up to a loft, which we used as a reading nook and yoga studio. That was something that both of us surprisingly really loved to do together. As high energy as Anna was, she loved yoga. I think it was a way for her to bring herself down in a calm and safe environment.

Living with her, I started to realize that she put a huge front up for people. She liked to be loud and obnoxious and high energy, but sometimes I got the feeling that she had a lot of deeper, darker stuff going on. I hadn't figured it out yet, and I didn't know if I ever would, but I just got the feeling. Yoga was a safe place for both of us to explore that side of ourselves with no judgments from anyone.

I had changed so much that year. I was nothing like the naive little girl who moved to Colorado to follow her loving boyfriend, and while sometimes I missed that girl, I was really impressed with the person I had become. When everything first happened, I didn't think that I would ever get over it, but here I was, on the other side, a stronger person. Stronger and also much more bitter, I thought, laughing at myself without any humor.

I turned the TV on, flipping until I found something mildly distracting. I still hated watching anything romantic, and thought that it was just a bunch of bullshit. If you were lucky enough to find someone you loved, ultimately the universe just took them from you. Better to just be by yourself. You couldn't get hurt that way. See what I mean about being bitter?

What I did love watching was really dark shit. Stuff like *Game of Thrones* and *The Handmaid's Tale*. It made me feel a little less depressed about my own life. Things that showed what life could really be like. Or at least my interpretation of life. Who knows, maybe other people did have the romantic, fluffy, happily-ever-after shit.

Anna walked in an hour later to find me finishing off the bottle of wine that I opened when I got home.

"Jesus, bitch. You couldn't have waited for me? Or even saved me any?"

"There's two more bottles on the counter, cunt," I said, laughing as she dashed into the kitchen to grab one for us.

"So, where are you in *Game of Thrones*?" Anna asked me as she came back in with an open bottle.

"I just watched the Red Wedding episode. In. Tense."

"Oh, girl, I told you you should've started way sooner. It's so good, right?"

"Well, I'm watching it now, bitch!"

"Don't you just love Khaleesi? God, she is so hot. I would gladly lick her pussy," Anna stated shamelessly.

"Anna!" I exclaimed, slightly stunned.

"What? Wouldn't you?"

"Ha! Well, I mean she is hot, but I've never wanted to go all lesbo with her or anything," I said. "I didn't know you were into girls." I looked at her questioningly.

"I'm not, really. I just have an enormous girl crush on her. She's just such a strong female character, and I love that."

"Well, I'm a strong female. Have you ever wanted to lick my hoo-ha?"

"Bitch, please. If you were ever to go into a fire and come out with three dragons draped over your naked body, then my answer would be yes, but since that hasn't happened yet, I would have to say no."

"Hey, who says I haven't?" I said, deadpan, before bursting out laughing a moment later.

We both stopped chatting and started another episode of *Game of Thrones*, making sure to drink lots of wine as we went.

"I'm starving," Anna said as the episode ended. "Pizza?"

"Oh, fuck yes," I said as we went into the kitchen to make our favorite, Totino's pepperoni pizza.

"So, I forgot to tell you. I went to the police station yesterday. I needed to see if they had any new info for me."

"And?" Anna asked.

"Nothing. Zero. They told me it's been way too long now. They gave up on the case months ago. They said that without a vehicle or any witnesses that they have absolutely no leads."

"Babe, I'm so sorry. So what are you going to do?"

"Well, at this point there's nothing I can do. I just need to let it go."

"Do you think you can do that?"

"I don't have a choice. I can't carry this with me anymore. It's eating me alive."

"Well, if I can help in any way, let me know."

"Thanks, Anna. You're a good friend," I told her sincerely.

"I know, I know," she said sarcastically. "So, on a lighter note, have you gotten your maid of honor dress yet?"

"No, not yet. I know I need to, but I am really dreading going into David's Bridal."

"Girl, I get it, but the wedding is not far off, and Savannah is freaking out a little about it. She keeps texting me over and over asking if you've gotten it."

"Fuck. Okay. I guess I've waited long enough. I was kinda hoping that if I didn't get it when she wanted me to that she would just kick me out of her wedding."

"Yeah, right! You know that would never happen. She would let you walk down the aisle in a potato sack before she would kick you out."

"Yeah, I know. Okay, well, I guess I'll go tomorrow since I have the day off."

"Oh, good! I have the day off too. Want me to come with you? I have some errands to run in the morning, but I can meet you there when I'm done," Anna asked.

"Really? Yes, I would actually love that."

"Yes, really. Even though I should make you go by yourself, since you have been absolutely zero help with the wedding stuff. You're the worst maid of honor ever," she teased, winking at me.

"Yeah, yeah. I know already," I said, rolling my eyes.

The next day, Anna and I met at the dress shop so I could finally get it all sorted out. She had beaten me there, and already had the dress ready for me, and as soon as I had it on and looked in the mirror, I busted out laughing. This had to be the ugliest dress on the face of the earth. It was poofy everywhere, including the shoulders, with tons of frills and lace, and it had the ugliest floral pattern I had ever seen.

"Is this really what we're wearing?" I asked Anna skeptically.

"No, it's what *you* are wearing. Mine is much sexier," she said seriously.

"You bitch. How did you convince her to put me in this?"

"I didn't," she said, laughing as she took a picture of me in the monstrosity. "Here's your real dress." She pulled out a much better dress from behind her back.

I laughed at her as I went back into the dressing room. The dress was very tight, but I managed to squeeze into it. This time when I looked in the mirror, I was pleasantly surprised. Typically when you had to be in the wedding party, you were forced to wear very unappealing dresses, probably to make the bride look even better, but Savannah made sure to pick very flattering dresses for both Anna and me.

The dress was burgundy and floor length. The top was all crocheted-looking lace with a deep V neckline and spaghetti straps. The top and waistline was fitted, before going down into a loose chiffon material on the bottom with a slit up the leg. I. Loved. It.

"We are also going to be wearing brown and tan furs over these during the ceremony since we will be outside in the middle of winter," Anna told me, making me love it even more.

One thing was for sure. This was going to be a beautiful wedding.

Chapter 5

Phoenix

It was the day of the wedding, and I was more nervous than the groom. I hadn't seen Lauren since riding in the ambulance with her. Did she remember anything? The hope she'd had? Our kiss? I bet she would hate me if she did. I barely knew her and I had already betrayed her trust. Or maybe she didn't even remember me at all. For some reason, I still had a strange, strong attraction to her. It felt wrong because of what she'd been through, but so right in a way I couldn't explain.

I was Charlie's only living groomsman. He was having Anna walk down the aisle alone, his best man being his dead brother. I thought it was very fitting, but that also meant that I would be walking down the aisle with Lauren. I was equally elated and anxious about it.

The couple was getting married at Spruce Mountain Ranch. Outside. While it was snowing. It had to have been a chic's idea, because they were clearly only thinking about how "pretty" it would look, when the reality was that we would all be freezing our asses off. Charlie was in all black, except for his suit jacket, which was burgundy with black lapels, and a black tie. My suit was all black with a burgundy tie.

"Hey, man. Let's take a shot," I said, holding out my flask of whiskey.

"Yeah right, man. If I get drunk, Savannah will kick my ass."

"Dude, just one shot. I have your back. I would never let you get trashed on your wedding day. Plus, if you think those girls aren't drinking too, you are dead wrong."

"Yeah, I guess you're right. They find any chance to drink and they grab it with both hands," Charlie said, chuckling fondly.

"Okay then. To marrying your better half," I said, holding up the flask and taking a swig before handing it off to Charlie.

He toasted before taking a generous gulp. "She is my better half. I knew on our first date that I was going to marry that frustrating, wonderful, smart, stubborn, beautiful woman."

"How did you know that from so early on?" I asked him.

"I can't explain it. I just did. I just felt more comfortable with her than I ever have with anyone else. And from the second I saw her in that bar, I was drawn to her."

Wow. That sounded familiar.

"We've had some rough times, of course, but I know that we can get through anything."

"Was there ever a time that you felt like you two weren't going to make it?" I asked.

"Just once. After my ex made it seem like I was cheating on her with Savannah. Other than that, no. We've had major fights, just like every couple, but after we cool down, I feel closer to her than I did before. What about you, man? Have you ever been in a relationship? I feel like I've never heard you talk about being with anyone before."

"Just one serious relationship. It was a long time ago."

I took another drink of whiskey as I thought about what he said. One thing was clear: I needed to ask Lauren out. I had to see if my feelings for her were real, or just some fluke, and I had a feeling that it wouldn't be an easy task.

Chapter 6

Lauren

"Hey, Lauren, would you grab me another mimosa, please?" Savannah asked sweetly as she was getting her makeup done.

"Sure, bride! Do you want peach, mango, or regular?"

"Peach, please."

I proceeded to make her drink and snag a few snacks before I brought it over to her. We were getting ready in the couples' hotel room. It was beautiful, especially the bathroom. It had a ginormous bathtub and a separate steam shower. We had hair and makeup come to us, which was really nice, because the wedding wasn't far from the hotel.

I had already gotten my hair done, and Anna was getting hers worked on and had already had her makeup finished. We decided to have Savannah get her hair and makeup done as late as possible so that it would last all day. So here I was, on my third mimosa already. I knew that as soon as the reception started, I would be drinking heavily, not wanting to let this wedding put me in a shit mood.

I was so excited and happy for the couple, but I couldn't get over the fact that this was supposed to be me. I was supposed to walk down the aisle and marry the love of my life and live happily ever after. I cried for a full hour when I woke up at the unfairness of it all. It had been a little while since I had done that. The only times in the last year that I had were on the anniversary of the accident, and on my due date. Both times, alcohol was the only thing that helped. Well, maybe not helped, but it sure as shit numbed the pain. Just like with today, and I needed to at least be able to act happy for Savannah. She deserved this. After the shit hand she got dealt in life, this was her karma. So I pasted a smile on my face, and took another drink of my mimosa as I brought her hers.

"I can't wait to see you in your dress after you get all put together, Savannah!" Anna exclaimed.

"Me neither! I've obviously seen it on during my fittings and stuff, but I haven't worn it since it's been altered. Plus, hair and makeup and jewelry will bring it all together," Savannah replied. She was doing a dark smoky eye with her eyeshadow, with a dramatic cat eye liner, and burgundy lipstick to match our dresses and her groom. Her hair would be put up in a low, messy bun, with a huge fishtail braid going back to join the bun and little tendrils hanging loose and curled around her face.

We were blaring some ghetto ass music to get in the mood for all the dancing later, including "Get Low" and "Apple Bottom Jeans." We also had just gone through a Tenacious D phase and listened to them for about a half hour.

"Okay, Lauren. You're up! Makeup time."

"Hey, as long as I can continue drinking, I am ready," I said as I plopped my ass down in the chair. I told the makeup artist that she could really do whatever she wanted with me, that I didn't want to think about it, and she got started. I almost had a panic attack when she put on the fake eyelashes, afraid that she was going to glue my eyes shut, but other than that, everything went smoothly. Before you knew it, we were all made up and looking gorgeous.

Anna and I put on our dresses before we helped Savannah with hers, figuring it would make things a bit easier. As soon as we had our dresses on, Savannah squealed and clapped her hands.

"Damn! You bitches are fine! And I picked out a damn good dress, if I do say so myself."

"Jesus, Lauren, you make me look like the ugly stepsister," Anna teased. "Nix isn't going to be able to keep his hands to himself as he walks you down that aisle."

I had forgotten that I had to walk down the aisle with that ridiculously good-looking man. My face felt like it paled and flushed all at the same time. For the first time in a long while, I felt that nervous, excited anticipation of seeing someone you might like. Then, I immediately felt guilty.

"Okay, bride, time to put on your dress!" Anna exclaimed, getting louder with each word in typical Anna fashion, and thankfully distracting me from my thoughts.

"Whew. Okay. Here we go," Savannah said, breathing slightly faster.

"Nervous?" I asked her.

"Yeah, a little. I don't know why though. It's not about marrying Charlie. I know that I want to spend my life with him, it's just that putting on the dress makes it feel so real. It almost didn't before."

"I know. I get the same way with big things. I remember the day that Ryan proposed. I knew he was going to do it, and it made me feel like I was going to throw up," I said, laughing and then tearing up at the end. Damn. It was moments like this where I had a hard time. If I didn't think about him or specific memories too much, I was okay. I took a deep breath to calm myself and force back the tears before continuing. "It's just because of all the anticipation of it. That's all. It's a big deal, and the body reacts the same way with anxiety and excitement. Sometimes it's hard to tell the difference. Once you see him, all the nerves will go away. Trust me." Savannah gave me a big

25

hug that I returned wholeheartedly, which was rare lately, but this day deserved it.

Once Savannah was in her dress, Anna and I stood back and took her in, both of us speechless for a moment.

"Well? Do I look okay?" she asked, uncertain.

"Girl. You. Look. Fantastic." And she did. She looked unlike any other bride I had ever seen. Her dress was very unique. It was a ball gown style dress. The bottom layer was all white and sleeveless, but the top layer was what made it so special. From the waist up was all black lace with long sleeves, and it cut down into a V-neck. From the waist down was just one layer of black tulle that covered all of the white. She then had a white fur stole over the dress for the ceremony. With her dark, dramatic makeup, she looked stunning. Just her style. To complete the look, she had a gorgeous leaf vine necklace with burgundy colored crystals that dropped down and accentuated the neckline of her dress perfectly, with earrings to match, of course.

"You look stunning, Savannah. Charlie will be speechless. And he's going to cry," I told her.

"Thank you, guys. I couldn't have done any of this without both of you. I love you both like sisters. You bitches *are* my sisters."

We all crowded in for a group hug and had our special moment before leaving for the wedding venue.

As we prepared to walk down the aisle, I took a moment to appreciate the beauty of where we were. It was basically a whole open field, the ceremony being held right next to a lake, with a view of the mountains in the background. The ground had a thin layer of snow, and big flurries were coming down, making it a winter wonderland.

The music started and Anna walked down by herself first. I took Nix's arm as we stood waiting for Anna to reach the front. I couldn't help but notice how strong and hard his arm was as he supported me.

"You look beautiful, Lauren," he said seriously, giving me a heated look. I felt a blush come to my cheeks as I smiled shyly at him.

"Thank you. You're not looking too bad yourself," I replied, surprising myself with my somewhat flirtatious response.

"I think it's our turn," Nix said with a smile in his voice. It was only then that I realized that I had been staring at him for longer than I should've been, and that he had noticed. My blush deepened as we started walking.

We got to the front and I gave Charlie an encouraging smile, and then the bride made her grand entrance. I heard the groom take a sharp inhale before I heard Nix lean over and say, "Just breathe, man."

The ceremony started, and I was finally able to enjoy the day and the couple. They were clearly so in love. It was mesmerizing to watch. A couple of times though, I would glance Nix's way, only to find him already staring at me. We locked eyes, and I didn't want to acknowledge the feelings that rose up inside of me.

Finally the words *I now pronounce you man and wife* broke the spell, and I looked toward the couple just in time to see the first kiss. We clapped and then it was time for us to walk back up the aisle. I once again clasped Nix's arm, holding on a little tighter than necessary. I felt like I needed to be anchored, like if I let go of him that I would float away.

"It's good to see you again," he said to me, speaking low enough that no one else could hear.

"Why's that?"

"I've wanted to see you again ever since that first time. I don't know why, but I'm drawn to you, Lauren." I was very surprised by his honesty and forwardness.

"The time you saw me with Ryan?" I asked, anger tinting my words.

"Yes. As soon as I knew you were taken, I adjusted my thinking, but even after all this time, I still haven't been able to get you out of my head." He paused and looked like he was debating what to say next. "I heard what happened, and I'm so sorry, Lauren."

"Yeah, well, thanks." By this time, we were down the aisle and I was torn between being royally pissed, and feeling an inexplicable pull toward him; his words had resonated with something deep inside me. Either way, as soon as I could, I yanked my hand away from his arm and tried to stalk off, only to have him grab my hand and pull me into him.

"Lauren, stop. I didn't mean to upset you. I shouldn't have said anything. I'm sorry," Nix whispered in my ear, the feeling of his breath on my neck making me shiver.

I took a deep breath before replying, but all that did was fill my nostrils with the delicious, manly scent of him, further messing with my mind. "It's fine. Just please don't mention Ryan to me. Especially not today, and not while you're touching me like this. It fucks with my head, and my head is already plenty fucked."

He chuckled before responding, "Understood."

I stepped away from him and made my way over to the happy couple, giving them both a big hug and offering my congratulations.

Anna, Nix, and I headed down to the lodge to make sure that everything was in order for the reception before everyone showed up. As soon as we finished, I went straight to the bar, ordering a huge glass of red wine. I took a grateful drink before I turned around and almost dumped the whole glass all over Nix's chest.

"Shit, sorry. I didn't realize you were right behind me. Why were you standing so close anyway?"

"I was just waiting to get a drink," he replied with the hint of a smile gracing his stupidly handsome face.

I nodded to him before walking off, taking another huge drink of my wine. I looked down at my glass to realize that it was already half empty. I rolled my eyes as I took my seat next to Anna. I almost groaned out loud when I saw Nix's name on the place card right next to mine. I was going to kill Savannah. I set down my wineglass way too hard on the table, almost breaking it in my frustration.

"What crawled up your ass?" Anna asked me.

"Nothing, I'm fine."

"Bitch, please. You know I live with you, right? Is it just the wedding?"

"Yeah, something like that," I mumbled.

"Hey, ladies," Nix said as he walked up to the table. "Do either of you see my name tag?"

"Yes," I answered, not looking at him, "it's right here." I glanced at Anna, only to find a knowing look in her eyes and a smile on her lips.

Fuck. Me. This was going to be a rough night, I thought as I took another drink.

Chapter 7

Phoenix

Lauren was so easily flustered by me. I took that as a good sign that maybe she had some similar feelings for me. As I took my seat next to her, I saw her glaring at Anna, who looked like she was trying to hold back a laugh. I pretended not to notice as I took a pull from my beer.

Soon people started filing in. Charlie and Savannah decided to have a sweetheart table instead of a head table, so the two of them were right in front of the huge fireplace, roaring fire included, and our table was right next to theirs, since we were basically their family.

The reception started, and the cheesiness commenced. It was a very nice wedding, but I wasn't a sentimental or romantic guy. The thing I did love about it was the free booze and the fact that I got to spend the night sitting next to Lauren, who was basically ignoring me, but still.

After dinner, the three of us gave our toasts, the couple had their first dance and cut the cake, and then the dancing started. By this time, Lauren and Anna were both fairly drunk, and I was also well on my way. Savannah came over to the table and dragged the girls away to dance with her.

"Come on, bitches! It's my wedding and 'Cha Cha Slide' is on. We have to dance," she said emphatically.

"Oh, fine!" Lauren gave in to Anna's and the bride's attempts. There was already a crowd of people on the dance floor, and once the ladies joined in, the whole group started dancing ridiculously.

I started laughing as I got up to join them. We danced and shouted through the whole song and I felt like I was in high school again. All of us were laughing by the end of it, and I saw a real smile on Lauren's face. I'm guessing it had been the first one in a long time. She was radiant.

I couldn't help myself. I was drunk and she was tempting. The next song started up, something slow, electronic, and sexy, and I made my way toward Lauren. I kept a little distance between us at first, but as soon as I saw her eyes blaze at me, I moved in to grind against her. She wrapped her arms around my neck as our gazes locked. The whole room disappeared, and it was just the two of us. I started to harden as her body moved against mine, and I almost lost my mind.

We continued to dance with each other for a handful of songs, and with each one that passed, I slowly felt her pussy getting hotter and wetter against me. By the fifth song, I couldn't take it anymore, and I kissed her with all of the sexual tension I felt. By the time the next song started, we were still kissing and our body movements had become more erratic.

Before I could get too carried away, however, the DJ announced the bouquet and garter toss. Lauren and I reluctantly broke away from each other as Anna pulled her toward the group preparing for the flower toss. Lauren looked fairly unenthusiastic about having to be part of it, but she participated anyway.

The bride centered herself on the dance floor before hurling the flowers behind her right into Lauren's arms. Lauren quickly tried to force them onto Anna, but Anna grabbed Lauren's arm and thrust it into the air, showing everyone who caught them, Everyone applauded as she glared at her friend.

Soon after, it was time for the garter toss. I sat firmly in my chair, planning on not participating, when the devil herself—you guessed it, Anna—walked up to me and forced me out of my seat and onto the dance floor to join the other men. As you probably have already guessed, Charlie flung the garter right into my hands, and I had to wonder if the whole thing had been planned.

Lauren and I found each other and started chuckling at the fact that we had both caught the items when neither wanted to participate in the first place. They played a slow dance next, and without asking, I wrapped her in my arms and whisked her around the dance floor.

"Where'd you learn to dance like this?" Lauren asked me.

"My parents made me take dance lessons when I was younger, no matter how strongly I protested," I replied.

"You, in dance lessons?!"

"Don't sound so shocked."

"You just don't seem like the type to ever do that, even at your parents insistence."

"Well, honestly, I never was going to, no matter how hard they pushed me, until my dad took me aside and told me that this would help me with the ladies eventually," I told her. "I thought until recently that he was full of shit."

"What changed your mind?"

"You did." She blushed and I leaned down to kiss her again.

The night wore on, and we continued to drink and dance our asses off. At the end of the wedding, we sent the happy couple off with lavender instead of rice, the party coming to a close.

"So, where are you headed?" she asked me.

"Well, I got a hotel room down the street because I knew I wasn't going to be sober enough to drive, so I was just going to walk there after the reception," I replied, leaning closer to her and running a finger over her exposed shoulder. "Want to come up with me?" I whispered in her ear, causing goosebumps to rise all along her shoulder, before kissing her neck directly underneath.

"Yes, Phoenix. Make me forget," she begged in my ear. Normally I didn't like people saying my full name, but on her lips it sounded sinful. I loved it.

I grabbed her hand and we made the quick five-minute walk to the hotel. Once we were in the elevator, I shoved her against the wall and ravaged her mouth, putting my leg in between both of hers. She moaned loudly as she ground her pussy against my thigh. The elevator doors opened, and I pulled her along behind me before clumsily opening my door. My mouth was on hers again before the door was even closed. I knew I was being frantic and a little crazy, but I couldn't help it. I had wanted her since I'd first laid eyes on her. Besides, it didn't seem like she minded because she was kissing me back just as fiercely and tearing at my clothes.

We both quickly undressed and my hands roamed over every inch of her body. Her breasts were perfect. I cradled both of them in my palms, teasing her nipples and smiling against her mouth when they pebbled between my fingers.

"Oh, Phoenix," she moaned. "I want you."

"Fuck, Lauren. I've wanted you since I first saw you," I told her as my fingers slipped between her pussy lips. "You're so wet," I growled, my control snapping.

She squealed when I threw her on the bed and climbed up after her. I kissed her before moving my lips down her body, eventually landing on her breasts. My fingers skated down her torso, causing goosebumps to follow in their wake. I took the tight bud of her nipple between my lips and sucked, plunging my finger into her wet heat at the same moment. By this time, she was squirming and moaning uncontrollably, her eyes slammed shut, absorbing all the sensations, and I thought it was the sexiest sight I had ever witnessed.

"God, baby, you're so tight."

"It's been a while," she told me, almost incoherently. Her eyes popped open, and for a moment I thought she was going to have me stop, but then I tugged her other nipple with my free hand and added another finger to her pussy and she settled back down, moving her hands into my hair to encourage me. "Phoenix, I need you inside me."

I growled my response against her skin, more than happy to oblige. I pulled away to grab a condom from my wallet, quickly slipped it on, and positioned myself at her entrance. I swiped my cock through her folds for a moment, coating myself in her wetness before thrusting inside her.

Heaven. That was the only way to describe how she felt wrapped around me. Not just my cock, but my entire being. Her legs were around my waist, her arms around my torso, her nails digging into my back, and her essence enveloping my soul. I paused for a second to take it all in, but before long, Lauren's heels were digging into my ass urging me on.

"Phoenix, I need you to move. Please," she begged me in a raspy whisper.

I pulled almost completely out before roughly plunging back in. At her cry, I pistoned my hips faster and harder, giving her all of myself. I knew in the back of my mind that I should be taking it slow and gentle with her, but I was drunk and my self-control when it came to her was sorely lacking. I brought my lips back to hers, and kissed her deeply. She bit my lip and tugged, and it unleashed the beast inside of me. We became wild in our movements, much like we did on the dance floor, and I knew this wouldn't last nearly as long as I needed it to.

"Oh God. I'm close. I'm going to come," she said frantically.

"Yes, Lauren. Come for me. I want to feel your greedy cunt milking my cock," I told her, doubling my efforts and rubbing my thumb against her clit, helping her along. Her nails scored my back and her scream pierced my ears as her orgasm ripped through her. The feel of the contractions on my dick sent me over the edge, and I spilled myself inside her.

Chapter 8

Lauren

I woke up the next morning too hot, with a blinding headache and the feeling that I was going to puke. I took a few deep breaths through my nose, and it settled my stomach just enough. Once I felt marginally better, I opened my eyes to find myself in an unfamiliar room. I looked behind me and discovered that the source of the heat that I was feeling was Phoenix. He was spooning me from behind, and we were both completely naked. All at once, the memories of the previous night came flooding back to me, and the nausea that had been at bay flickered to life again in my stomach.

I couldn't believe I had slept with Phoenix. From what I remember, it was phenomenal, but the thought that had my gut churning was the fact that I had slept with someone besides Ryan, and worse, I had enjoyed it. Tears gathered in my eyes, but I couldn't cry now. I had to get out of bed and out of this room before Nix woke up. From the sound of his light snoring, I didn't think it would be that hard of a task.

I carefully moved his arm off of my torso, and crawled slowly out of bed. When I was confident that he had not woken, I quickly grabbed my clothes from the floor and made my way to the bathroom. Once I relieved my bladder and put on my dress from the wedding, I snuck back into the room and to the door, glancing behind me. Nix was still sleeping soundly in bed, and I had a twinge at the thought of leaving him. I knew he was going to be pissed, I would be, but I couldn't do this. I wasn't ready.

I walked into the apartment to find Anna already awake and watching TV on the couch with a cup of coffee.

"Hey, you dirty little slut," she greeted me.

"Oh, hey. You're up early."

"No I'm not. You were just hoping I was still sleeping so you wouldn't have to deal with my interrogation."

"Yes, you're right. So, on that note, I'm gonna go take a shower."

"Oh, hell no. What happened? Last I saw, you and Nix were swallowing each other's tongues and dry humping the shit out of each other on the dance floor. Since you're still wearing your maid of honor dress, I'm going to assume you fucked his brains out? Also, on a side note, I'm pretty pissed you left without letting me know." Well, so much for sneaking in and not talking about last night ever.

"Yeah, we slept together," I admitted, a blush creeping up my cheeks. "And I'm sorry that I didn't tell you. I was pretty fucking drunk if you didn't notice."

"Yeah, all the more reason to let me know where you were going. I was pretty worried about you," she snapped at me. "That's how people get abducted and raped and murdered and shit."

"Look, Anna, I'm sorry. I just wasn't thinking. I got caught up in the moment with Nix and didn't think to tell you."

"It's okay. I'm sorry I snapped at you, I just didn't sleep that well, and I've been a little worried," she apologized, and then forced a cheerful look to her face. "So, how was it?"

"Well, the act itself was incredible," I sighed, "but this morning, not so much."

"Give me details, bitch! Stop making me ask," Anna yelled at me, making me wince from the pounding in my head.

"Well, we got back to the hotel, and we were pretty quick in getting to it, but we were both super drunk. Then I woke up hungover as shit this morning and snuck out before he could wake up."

"Oh, shit. You didn't wake him up?"

"No! Of course I didn't wake him. I feel like shit about sleeping with him. I should never have done that. I can't see him again, and I didn't want to tell him that and make him feel like shit."

"And leaving before he wakes up is supposed to make him feel less shitty?"

"Fuck. I'm too hungover for this. I just couldn't deal with it this morning, okay?" I snapped at her.

"Okay, girl. I'm sorry. I didn't mean to make you feel bad about it," she said. "Why don't you think you can see him again?"

"Why do you think, Anna? He isn't Ryan. I feel so guilty. I haven't slept with anyone new in seven fucking years."

"Baby, I know, but you have to move on eventually. It's not like you cheated on Ryan. He's gone, honey. He would want you to find someone else."

"Well, I don't want to find someone else. I just want Ryan," I said, defeated, and then immediately felt guilty again, because I knew it was a lie. I could already feel the pull toward Nix and I'd had only one night with him. "I'm done talking about this. I'm going to take a shower and then go back to bed."

"Okay, girl. Just don't beat yourself up about it, okay? I know that maybe you aren't quite ready yet, but don't write Nix off completely. He's a good guy," Anna told me, getting off the couch to give me a tight hug. I nodded at her before walking off.

I hopped into the shower, letting the hot water relax my tight muscles. I watched the water run over my body and down the drain, imagining it washing away the night's events along with my guilt and anxiety. I wasn't sure how long I stood there, the water cleansing my conscience, but by the time the water ran cold, I suddenly knew what I was going to do next. The answer I had been searching for, for years, was now right in front of my face, flashing like a neon sign.

I got out of the shower with a new sense of purpose. I smiled to myself when I realized that I felt better than I had in a long time.

Chapter 9

Phoenix

I woke up with a satisfied feeling deep in my bones, despite how hungover I was. I rolled over and stretched deeply, letting a contented sigh fall from my mouth. My eyes popped open as soon as I remembered the events of the night before.

"Lauren?" I called out. No answer. The room was completely silent except for my breathing.

I got up and checked to see if maybe she was in the bathroom, even though I doubted she was. Finding it empty, I walked back to bed, tripping over my clothes on the way there, and realizing Lauren's clothes were missing.

So it was official, she'd bailed. I didn't know why I was surprised at that, but I was, and very disappointed. Last night had been amazing, at least I thought so, but it appeared that she didn't.

It was my own stupid fault. I should never have invited her up here. I knew that she wasn't ready for it, but I couldn't help it. Between the drinks and the fact that I had thought about her for over a year, it was a dangerous combination. I wished I could have a do-over with her to get things right. To treat her like a lady and take her out on a date, but

I didn't know if I would get that chance. I didn't even have her fucking number. I rolled my eyes at the thought. Figures. I would sleep with an amazing woman and I wouldn't even get her information so I could call her.

A thought popped into my head. I bet I could get it from Charlie. He wouldn't give it to me at first, but maybe after some pestering he would. Of course, I wouldn't see him for a while since he was away on his honeymoon, but maybe that was a good thing. It would give Lauren time to calm down, and me time to come up with a strategy.

With that plan in place, I went back to sleep for a few hours, dreaming of a time when Lauren would be mine.

Two weeks later...

It was one of those weird Colorado days, where it was the middle of winter, but it was sixty degrees outside, so I decided to ride my motorcycle into work. It felt amazing. I always hated the winter, just for the simple fact that I couldn't ride my bike. I inwardly smiled as I took off, feeling the wind whip at my face and hair.

My mood was very light. Not only was I able to ride to work, but it was Charlie's first day back from his honeymoon. I was sure that I could get Lauren's number off of him, which meant that I would be able to hopefully talk to her tonight.

I walked in the front door to see all the guys crowding around Charlie, patting him on the back and asking him how his trip was. I grabbed both of us a cup of coffee before joining them and handing it to him, figuring that he hadn't been able to get there yet due to the mob surrounding him. He took a big gulp before giving me a grateful smile.

"So, how was Greece, man?" I asked.

"Dude, it was phenomenal. So much delicious food and wine."

"Where were you exactly again?"

"Santorini and Mykonos were the islands we stayed on. Santorini was our favorite though. We could've stayed there the whole time, but Mykonos was really amazing too. Plus Savannah wanted to have some beach time, and that's what that island is known for."

For the next half hour, Charlie told us stories, and showed us a plethora of pictures, before a call finally came in. We quickly all suited up and got onto the truck. On the way to our location, Charlie nudged me with his elbow. "Hey, so I saw you and Lauren at the wedding. You guys were climbing down each other's throats. Did anything happen?" he asked.

"That night, yes, but when I woke up the next morning, she had bolted. Me, being the dumbshit I am, didn't get her phone number that night either, so I haven't even been able to contact her," I replied, hoping that maybe he would just offer it up to me.

"Damn, that's pretty brutal. Can't say I blame her though. She's been through so much shit."

"Yeah, I know. I wouldn't have made a move on her, or at least not taken her to bed if I was sober, but we both were pretty trashed."

"I totally get it, man, but she just probably needs some time and space to settle her conscience."

"I know," I replied, getting slightly frustrated. He was telling me stuff I already knew, but I needed to talk to Lauren. I didn't like how we left things and I wanted to make sure she was all right. "Do you have her number?" I was going to try to be smoother than that, but apparently that was all the coaxing I had in me.

"Well, of course I do, but that doesn't mean I'm going to give it to you. Savannah would have my balls, dude."

"Come on. Please?" I gritted out through my teeth.

"Damn. You must really want it. I don't think I've ever heard you ask nicely," he mocked me.

"Fuck off."

"Now that's more like it," he laughed. "Okay, I'll give it to you, but be respectful, and if you tell her I gave it to you, I'll sic my wife after you."

"Deal."

I got home after a long day and immediately opened up a beer. I decided to take it into the shower with me to help settle my nerves about texting Lauren. I didn't even remember the last time I was nervous about texting a girl. High school maybe?

I quickly dried off and opened my messages. Unsure of what to say, I stared at the screen for about five minutes, hoping that the answer would just suddenly magically appear on my phone. Finally, deciding to keep it light, I texted her.

Hey, stranger.

Who is this? she texted a moment later.

Jesus. Of course she didn't know who it was and I ended up sounding creepy. I rolled my eyes at my own stupidity.

Nix.

Oh. Hey.

So, you disappeared the other morning?

As soon as I sent it, I questioned whether I was already pushing her too hard. I saw that she had read the text, but she still hadn't replied. I waited, leaving the app open, willing her to say something. Finally, after about five minutes, or what felt like five minutes, three little dots appeared.

I know. And I'm sorry. I had a really fun time the other night, but it was too much for me.

I shouldn't have asked you up to my room. I thought it was probably too soon for you, I just had too much to drink and you were irresistible.

You were pretty irresistible too...

Would you want to get together soon? Purely innocent. I promise.

Phoenix...

Yes, Lauren?

I can't. Not yet at least. I need to get my shit together. And I'm not there yet.

Okay, I can respect that. But will you at least agree to give me a chance when you feel ready?

Yes. I will definitely agree to that.

Deal. And I also reserve the right to text you occasionally.

Haha. Okay. Deal.

I went to sleep that night with a smile on my face.

Chapter 10

Lauren

Three months later...

"The light and dark inside of me honors the beautiful light and dark inside each of you. Together we are one. Namaste," I breathed, closing the class.

All of the students returned my bow before collecting their yoga mats and water bottles and filing out of the room.

Anna came up to me as soon as everyone else had left.

"Girrrrrrl. That was such a good class!" she exclaimed, making me blush slightly under the praise.

"Really? Did I do okay for my first one?"

"Yes, babe. It was fantastic. I know it was free because you are a new teacher, but I would've paid for that shit." I smiled at her before we both went to the lobby of the studio. "I'm going to shower while you kick everyone out. Then we can make out before we drive home together." She winked at me, making me laugh before she went into the locker room.

Since the class had been free, there were actually quite a few people who came. There were around ten or so including Anna, which was a pretty decent-sized class. I had originally been very nervous that there were so many people there, but then again, if it had just been Anna and me, I would've been pretty disappointed.

"Hey, great class!" one of the ladies commented on her way out of the studio.

"Thank you!" I shouted at her, probably a little too loudly, but I was excited that someone besides Anna enjoyed it.

I got a few more comments as people left, and twenty minutes later, the doors were locked and I was waiting on Anna. Another ten minutes passed before she came out of the locker room, freshly showered and makeup done.

"Bitch, what took you so long? Also, you don't need to do your fucking makeup, we're just going home!" I yelled at her when she came out.

"I wanted to look good for you when we make out," she teased, chuckling. "Girl, you know I don't like to leave the house without makeup on."

"Fair enough. Well, since you're all dolled up, wanna go to dinner or something?" I asked, realizing how hungry I was.

"Hell yes. Do you even need to ask?"

"Well, where do you want to go?"

"Sushi?" she asked.

"Yes. Let's do Sushi Hai."

We got to the restaurant, and were sat at a two-seater table, complete with cushions on the ground instead of chairs. We both ordered martinis and edamame for an appetizer. Once those came we put in our sushi order, probably ordering way too much for just the two of us, but we knew we would eat it all.

"So, how do you feel about your first class?" Anna asked me as we waited for our food.

"I feel like it went really well. I was pretty nervous at first, but then

I settled in and it just felt so right. Like this is what I've always been meant to do."

"That's fantastic. I know how you've been really unhappy at your job lately."

"It's not that I've been unhappy necessarily, just that I don't want to do hair anymore. Plus, I really wanted to find my calling, or whatever the fuck it is that people call it."

"Well, based on that class, you definitely found it."

"Thanks, lady. You're always brutally honest, so I know you're telling me the truth," I stated, laughing. "I feel so good. I don't think I've felt this good since before the accident. Even then, I was super happy with Ryan and my life with him, but I haven't been content in my career for years. I feel like I'm finally coming into myself and discovering who I'm supposed to be."

"Oh, honey. That makes me so happy to hear. It was hard watching you struggle like you did and not be able to really do anything for you."

"You did more than you know, Anna. You've always had my back, and you took me in when you knew I shouldn't be by myself. You saved me from myself. I can never thank you enough," I voiced sincerely.

Anna blushed slightly under the praise, before giving a typical Anna response. "Well, it was all so I could see you naked around my apartment, which of course still hasn't happened," she joked as I rolled my eyes and chuckled.

Our sushi came, and we stuffed our faces and washed it down with our drinks. When we had finished all of our rolls and both of our martinis I started another subject with her that I was feeling pretty excited about.

"So, I think I'm ready to get together with Phoenix."

A strange look crossed Anna's face, but it was gone so quickly I figured I had imagined it. "Oh yeah? That's a big deal."

"Yeah. I think I finally feel ready. I was waiting to feel steady and stable in myself as a person, and I think I'm at that point now."

"Have you guys talked at all since Savannah's wedding?"

"Just a little bit. Some innocent get-to-know-you type stuff."

"He's a pretty great guy, huh?" Anna asked.

"He really is. Honestly, I never expected him to want to talk to me after I ditched him, but he was very understanding about it."

"So, are you going to ask him on a date then?"

"I wasn't sure what to do. What do you think?" I asked. I hadn't been in a situation like this in a long time. I felt like I was back in high school.

"I think you should. Guys like it when women are forward and make the first move. Which, I mean, isn't technically true, since you already slept together, but you get the idea." She winked at me and laughed.

"Bitch," I muttered under my breath, winking back at her.

We paid the tab and drove back to our apartment. We put a girly movie on before calling it a night and heading to bed. I lay in bed, my message thread to Nix open as I debated on what to text him. Finally, I decided to just keep it straightforward.

Wanna go out on a date with me? I'm ready now.

His response was almost instantaneous.

Yes. Is tomorrow too soon?

No. Tomorrow's perfect!

Five?

Yes :)

Don't wear anything fancy.

His response confused and intrigued me. I would have figured he'd want to take me out to a nice dinner or something.

Whatever you say, sir.

Don't call me sir. It does things to me...

Well, in that case, yes sir.

Lauren...

I'll see you tomorrow...sir.

I put my phone on silent and went to sleep laughing as I pictured how he would respond.

Chapter 11

Phoenix

I knocked on Lauren's door the next day, both excited and nervous at the same time. I smoothed out my shirt while waiting for her to answer. I wore a pair of dark jeans, a dark gray T-shirt and my black leather jacket. Twenty seconds later, the door opened with a glorious-looking Lauren on the other side of it. She was wearing black skinny jeans, ratty black Converse, a tank top that said "Fuck Everything and Become a Pirate," and a leather jacket. Her hair was pulled up into a messy bun on the top of her head. She looked absolutely beautiful. There was something about a woman in ratty rocker clothes that made me hard as fuck. Or maybe it was just Lauren. Probably that one.

I leaned in to kiss her cheek in greeting. "You look stunning, Lauren," I whispered in her ear as I pulled back.

I saw her blush before she said, "You're full of shit, but thanks."

"I'm definitely not. Are you ready to go?"

"Yep!"

I grabbed her hand and led her down to where my bike was parked on the side of the street, and handed her a helmet.

She looked down at the helmet and then back at the bike before an anxious look crossed her face.

"Have you ever ridden on a motorcycle before, Lauren?" I asked, thinking that's why she was nervous.

"I actually have. Many times. My dad had a bike when I was growing up and he would take me out on it a lot," she said, but that look stayed firmly planted on her face.

"Well, then why are you nervous, babe?"

"I haven't been on one in a long time, and with the accident, it just makes me even more anxious to be on the road."

Jesus. Christ. I hadn't even thought of that. I was such an ass.

"Fuck, Lauren. I am so sorry. I'm such an idiot. I can go home and get my car instead."

"No. Don't. I want to go for a ride. I love riding. It just makes me a little nervous is all. I'll be fine once we get moving."

"Are you sure?" I asked, stroking my thumb down her cheek and looking into her eyes, as if they would give me the answers.

"Yes. I'm sure." And with that, she put her helmet on, looking even cuter if that was possible.

"All right then," I said, putting my own helmet on and getting on my bike. Once I was situated, Lauren climbed on, pressing herself against me and wrapping her arms tightly around my torso. I put my hand on top of both of hers for a couple seconds, enjoying the feeling of her warmth.

I started my bike, and we were off. I could tell that she had ridden before. She leaned when I leaned, moving with me as opposed to most newbies who tended to lean the opposite way, which always made it more difficult. I went slow at first, taking it easy on Lauren, but after a few minutes, she shouted "Faster!" in my ear, so I gave her what she wanted, and before long, we were in Golden.

After we parked and got off the bike, I looked back at Lauren to see a huge smile on her face.

"Wow. That was so much fun. I forgot how much I love riding. I haven't been in so long."

I smiled at her as I got the little picnic I had packed for us out of my back compartment. I then grabbed her hand as we started walking. I wanted to find the perfect spot for us.

"So, what have you been up to recently?" I asked her as we strolled along.

"Well, I recently just finished my yoga teacher training. I taught my first official class yesterday."

"Oh really? That's awesome. Are you still cutting hair?"

"For now. All my classes are free right now since I'm just starting out, but hopefully once I get my name out there, I'll be able to quit and just do yoga."

"Good for you, Lauren. It takes a lot of guts to pursue a new path like that. Especially getting away from what you're used to."

"What about you? Have you always wanted to be a fireman?"

"I don't know. My dad was a fireman, so I guess I took after him."

"Do you enjoy it?" she asked.

"Honestly, I've never really thought about it. I just do it. My dad always wanted me to follow in his footsteps," I said, this conversation making me think about things I wasn't sure I wanted to.

"Well, are there any hobbies that you love doing on your own?"

"Yeah. I actually really love working with wood. I made a lot of the furniture around my house."

"Wow, really? That's amazing. I would have no idea how to even go about that."

"I got into it in high school. I took a shop class and I loved it. I eventually saved up some money and started to buy my own tools," I told her, reliving that first class I took.

"Have you ever sold any of it?" she asked.

"No. I've always just done it for myself."

"Well, maybe you should try it. I bet you could really do something with that if you ever wanted to get out of what you're doing now. Or just as a side income. People love buying shit on Etsy, me included."

"Well, maybe you'll be my first customer," I teased her.

"I would be honored, sir," she whispered, winking at me.

I groaned. Hearing her call me that in person in that throaty voice of hers made me want to do things to her that she was not ready for yet, if our last encounter was any indication. She laughed loudly at me, I'm sure following the direction my thoughts had taken. She had the most beautiful laugh. It was so full and melodic.

Just then, we came upon a little clearing. It had a creek running through it, trees surrounding it, and wildflowers all over.

"What about this spot?" I asked her.

I heard her sharp inhale as she looked around. "Oh my God. This is perfect. It looks like it's right out of a Bob Ross painting," she breathed.

She was right. It was gorgeous. We picked a spot next to the creek, I spread out a blanket, and we sat down before I started getting out all the food that I had packed. I had bought fried chicken from the deli at the grocery store, as well as mac and cheese, mashed potatoes and gravy, and rolls. I also brought us a couple of beers. I opened us each one and held my bottle up to hers in cheers. We settled in to eat, neither of us talking for a while, just admiring the beauty of where we were.

When we were finished eating, I asked her, "So, why don't you have crazy colors in your hair anymore?" It was a question that had been burning in my brain ever since I saw her with her natural hair color at the wedding.

She looked at me before sighing and taking a big swig of beer. "My hair has been a different color every day since I turned thirteen. I had always thought that it was an outward expression of my personality." She paused, looking out over the water before continuing. "When I had my miscarriage and Ryan passed, I felt like that part of myself had died right along with them. At that point I didn't feel like that colorful, life-loving, happy person existed anymore. That was one of the first things I changed after the accident. As soon as I was able to get out of bed and go about my 'life,' I dyed it my natural, boring hair color."

"For the record, I don't think that it's boring at all, it just doesn't feel like you. Do you think you'll ever change it back?" I asked.

"You know, I'm just starting to get the urge again, although I don't think I'll go as crazy as I did before the accident. I might do like a dark brown with streaks of something vivid. I haven't decided yet."

"Well, whatever you decide to do will look beautiful on you," I told her as I tucked a stray tendril of hair behind her ear, loving the way a blush crept up her cheeks. We locked eyes and had a moment where I felt like we could see into each other's souls. I leaned in closer to her just as she did the same. We both moved very slowly as if savoring the moment. Just as our lips brushed and I could feel her breath on my face, a dog came running by us, barking and splashing into the water. We quickly broke apart, startled.

"Shadow! Get back here!" some lady yelled as she ran after her dog. "Oh, I'm so sorry, guys. I didn't know there was water back here, and once he smells it, he can't control himself."

"That's okay!" Lauren assured her. "How old is he?"

"He's two years old. I got him from a shelter when he was six months old. He's usually really calm and great off leash, but he loves water," she replied, just as Shadow came out of the water to stand next to her. "Well, have a good night, guys!" she said, continuing her hike. We looked at each other and awkwardly chuckled at being interrupted.

"Ooh, look, the sun's going down," Lauren said excitedly.

We both leaned back on the blanket side by side and watched the sunset. After a few minutes, I put my hand over hers next to me. She glanced at me and gave me a warm smile before turning her attention back to the view.

When there was officially no more light, we packed everything up and made the trek back to my bike. We hopped on and I savored the feeling of Lauren pressing against me once more before I took off. I went a little faster this time since she seemed more comfortable, and from the sound of her squeals and the way she gripped me tighter and laughed, I would say she liked it.

All too soon, we were pulling up to her apartment, and her warmth was missing from my back. I walked her to her door, both of us stalling, not wanting the night to end.

"I had a really nice time tonight, Phoenix. Thank you," she said as she leaned in closer to me.

"I'm glad, Lauren. I had a great time too." I leaned even closer, wanting a redo on our missed kiss from earlier. She let me. I started slowly, just brushing my lips across hers, but it soon turned heated. I deepened it to find her tongue already seeking mine. We both fought for control, but I eventually won. When we were both breathless, I pulled back and rested my forehead against hers.

"Wanna come in?" Lauren asked breathlessly.

"I would fucking love to. But I don't think you're ready for that yet. Last time we really rushed things, and I don't want to do that this time. I'm not in this just for one night, Lauren. I want you, but I want you when you're ready for me," I said, stroking her cheek.

"Well, you sure do know how to make a girl swoon," she chuckled.

"Until next time, sweetness," I whispered, leaning in to give her one more kiss.

Chapter 12

Lauren

One week later...

It was the game to determine who would be in the playoffs. The Packers or the Lions. Being from Michigan, I was a Lions fan, even though most of the time it was very difficult, but this year we were actually doing fairly decent.

I watched the games religiously every week, just like my dad taught me to. The only problem was that I never had anyone to watch them with. Anna hated sports and always left the room whenever I turned the game on. Savannah and Charlie weren't football fans. Savannah never used to watch sports at all until Charlie introduced her to his favorite sport: lacrosse. This Sunday, however, I had a fantastic idea.

Hey, wanna come over and watch the Lions stomp the Packers?

I sat there, anxiously awaiting a response. Luckily I didn't have to wait long for three little dots to appear, signaling a reply.

Umm, please. The Packers are going to kick their ass so bad.

So, is that a yes?

Well, I would love to see you and watch the game with you, but I have plans to watch the game with my family already. You should come over here and watch with us.

Hmm. Meet his family already? Wasn't it a little soon? Plus, I would be the only Lions fan in a Packers household. That didn't bode well for me. However, I would get to see Phoenix, and watch the game with football fans.

Really? Your family won't kick me out when I show up in my jersey, will they?

Only if your team ends up winning... ;)

Fair enough. Where and when?

I showed up to Nix's house at 2:00 p.m. on the dot, wearing my number nine Matthew Stafford jersey. The game started at 2:30, so that gave me time to meet everyone before we were immersed in it.

His house was absolutely beautiful. At least from the outside. It was in an old neighborhood, complete with classic Victorian houses. It was light green, almost blue, with a gray roof and white trim. In the peak, there were fish scales that were a dark, almost forest green color and lots of ornamentation. Needless to say, it was my dream house and I was officially jealous.

My stomach was full of butterflies as I knocked on the door. Nix answered seconds later, sporting a number twelve Aaron Rodgers jersey, and looking delicious.

"Hey, sweetness! You look beautiful. Come on in," he said, leaning in to give me a kiss. It was probably meant to be quick, but as soon as our lips touched, I opened my mouth for him. He groaned as his tongue came out to meet mine. A throat cleared behind him and I jumped back, embarrassed at being caught.

"Mrs. Narrow, it's so nice to meet you!" I said, rushing forward with my hand out, trying to back-pedal after being caught with my tongue down her son's throat. I inwardly rolled my eyes at myself. What a first impression.

Nix's mom, a middle-aged woman with dark brown hair and a kind face, batted my hand away and quickly wrapped me in a hug. "Lauren, I'm so glad you could come over today. We've all been dying to meet the woman that Phoenix can't stop talking about. And please, call me Caroline." I loved her instantly. She reminded me of my mom, and immediately made me feel at home.

"Ma, don't overwhelm her, she just got here," Phoenix said, coming up behind me to put a hand on my back.

"Oh, shush. We're best friends already, aren't we, Lauren?" she asked, looking at me expectantly.

"Of course, Caroline," I said, putting my arm around her, making her laugh loudly.

"Oh, I like this one already, Phoenix. I can see why you're so taken with her. Let's go into the living room to meet everyone," she said, dragging me along with her. Nix's face turned red at her comment, but he followed along behind us quietly. "Everyone come meet Lauren!" she shouted as soon as we entered.

I was soon surrounded by three huge, red-haired men, all in Packers jerseys. "Hi, everyone, I'm Lauren Spekter. Thank you all so much for letting me crash the Packers party." Nix finally came up next to me to extract me from his mother's arms and introduce me to his family.

"Lauren, this is my dad, Bill. He was a firefighter for thirty years before he got injured and had to retire," Nix told me, and I shook Bill's hand and told him it was nice to meet him. "These are my younger brothers, Griffin and Lincoln." I shook their hands as well, before admiring the four strong male presences before me. It was insane how similar they all looked. They were carbon copies of their older, good-looking father.

"Wow, I can see who Nix takes after, appearance wise, well, and career wise."

"Yes, all three of my boys are serving in some way. Phoenix for the fire department, Griffin for the police, and Lincoln in the Coast Guard. I'm, of course, so proud of them, but it would be nice if they had careers that didn't make their only mother worry so much," Caroline chastised fondly.

"I can imagine. I wouldn't want my children doing such dangerous jobs either," I added, making all the men roll their eyes and Caroline smile and tell me that she knew she liked me for a reason. "So, on a lighter note, I brought homemade French onion dip if anyone wants to try it," I said, taking the pressure off the guys.

"Oh, yes. My favorite," Bill said, immediately taking it from me and digging in.

"Lauren, honey, would you like something to drink? We have beer, and I also make a mean Bloody Mary," Caroline asked, ever the hostess, I assumed.

"Yes, please. I love Bloodys. Extra spicy if you can."

After that, we settled in for the game, booze and all sorts of food in front of us. As far as the two teams went, we were pretty evenly matched throughout the whole thing, and while I had originally felt somewhat out of place being the only Lions fan, I soon felt very comfortable and really enjoyed watching the game with them. We occasionally gave each other shit, but it was all in fun.

It was the end of the fourth quarter, and the Lions were up by a touchdown. There were only twenty seconds left in the game. I, of course, started gloating.

"Well, it was a nice try, you guys, but it looks like we're going to the playoffs this year."

"Not so fast, little lady," Bill said. "There are still twenty seconds left in the game and we have the ball. Never count your chickens before they hatch. Especially when it comes to Aaron Rodgers."

I rolled my eyes, right until the play started. Before I knew it, Rodgers was throwing a Hail Mary into the end zone. We all held our breath, waiting to see if anyone would catch it. Sure enough, Davante Adams jumped as high as he could and snagged the ball in the end zone. Phoenix's family erupted in cheers, and I was left sitting on the couch, speechless.

"Told ya, darlin', don't underestimate us," Bill said, winking at me.

With that, the game went into overtime, and the Packers won by a touchdown, having found their momentum with the last play.

"Well, I didn't want you guys to win, but I have to admit that was a fuckin' helluva play," I told the room once the game was over.

"It was a nice try, Lauren, but it looks like we're going to the playoffs this year," Nix said, quoting me from earlier.

I bumped against him. "Oh, shut up," I said, laughing.

The next few hours were spent eating, talking, getting to know each other, and drinking a shit ton. I thought I could drink, but his family was drinking me under the table. After too many drinks to count, I said as much.

"Jesus, how the hell do you guys drink so much? I thought I could keep up, but I'm ready to pass out and you guys don't seem to be even tipsy."

"Oh, honey. We're from Wisconsin. We're all fairly drunk, but we know how to hide it well and keep going," Caroline told me.

"Speak for yourself, lass. I don't get drunk," Bill slurred slightly as he smacked his wife on the ass.

"When did you all move out here?" I asked. No wonder they were all such die-hard Packers' fans, and why Caroline made such good Bloody

Marys.

"When I was fifteen," Phoenix spoke up next to me, his hand on my back. He seemed to really like touching me. Ever since the accident, I hated people touching me, but with him, I loved it. I soaked up every brush of his fingers and every supporting hand. It was like there was an electric current running from him into me, and it was restoring me bit by bit.

Phoenix must have picked up on my train of thought, because we suddenly locked eyes and everything became very heated. I licked my lips and his gaze zeroed in on my mouth. Just as we were about to lean in for a kiss, his brothers started arguing loudly about politics.

"Oh, God. I thought they had stopped this shit," Phoenix mumbled under his breath. "Every time they get drunk together they end up debating for hours."

"Do either of them ever change their mind?"

"Nope," he told me, laughing.

"Well, on that note, I should probably head home. I have to work early tomorrow," I said with regret. It had been a perfect night. His family reminded me so much of mine that I immediately felt at home.

"Are you okay to drive?" he asked me.

"Definitely not, but I got an Uber here because I knew I would be drinking."

"Can I give you a ride home?"

"You've been drinking too."

"Not for the last few hours. I saw how much you were drinking and I thought this would be my opportunity to get you alone," he joked, grabbing my hand and pulling me toward the door. "Hey, everyone, I'll be right back. I'm going to drive Lauren home."

"Hey, let me say goodbye to everyone first!" I said, giggling. He was in such a hurry to be alone with me.

I hugged all of his family members, although his dad was slightly awkward at it, but his mom made up for it, wrapping me in a tight and warm embrace.

We finally made it out of the house, and Nix drove me home, holding on to my hand the entire way. He parked and got out of the car to open my door and walk me to my apartment.

"Thanks for letting me be a part of this wonderful day. Your family is amazing," I told him.

"Yeah, they're pretty great. And for the record, they love you."

"Really? How do you know?"

"They all told me when you went to the bathroom. Especially my mom. She already asked me when we're getting married," he said, chuckling.

"I loved her too, she reminds me a lot of my mom. Except a little louder," I said fondly, smiling.

"You know what we should do someday?" Nix asked me suddenly.

"No, what?"

"We should go to a Packers Lions game at Lambeau Field."

"Oh, I would love that! I've never been to a live game before, and I've heard that that stadium is fantastic!" I exclaimed, very excited at the thought.

"Good. It's a date." Nix cupped my face in his hand before leaning in to capture my lips with his. With the buildup from earlier, it didn't take long before it became heated. He pinned me up against the wall and started grinding himself into me. I could feel his erection pressed against my belly and I moaned low in my throat, grinding against him harder. His hands made their way to my breasts, and just as he bit my lip, the front door opened.

We jumped apart, having been caught again. Anna stood on the other side of the door, first looking startled, and then annoyed.

"Oh, sorry to interrupt. I heard something and thought I'd check it out," she said testily before shutting the door, leaving us to ourselves again.

"It seems like we can never be intimate without being interrupted," I commented.

"It's the universe telling me you still aren't ready," Nix teased.

"Oh, believe me, if you put your hand in my panties, you would find out how ready I am."

"Babe, don't put that image in my head while I'm in this state. I won't be able to take it slow with you like I'm really trying to," Nix groaned in my ear.

"Okay, well then get out of here before I drag you inside with me," I said, swatting him on the ass.

He gave me another quick kiss before taking off.

I opened the front door to find Anna on the couch watching TV.

"Hey. Sorry if we startled you. He was just walking me to the door," I told her, feeling the need to apologize since she seemed to be fairly annoyed about it.

"Oh, just walking you to the door, huh? It looked like a helluva lot more than that to me." Her tone caught me off guard, and I was unsure how to respond.

"Uh, well, he walked me to the door and then gave me a good-night kiss. Why are you so upset, Anna?"

"Well, you startled me. I was worried there was someone sketchy outside. Plus, I feel like I never see you anymore. You work, you were taking your classes, you're going to be teaching, and now you're spending the rest of your free time with Nix," she said, starting out defensive, and then morphing into slightly whiny at the end.

"We didn't mean to startle you. I'm sorry. And I'm also sorry that I've been so busy lately. I'm trying to get my life back in order, Anna."

"I know you are. I just miss you. I live with you, but I never see you. I thought we could've spent the day together since we were both off, but then you disappeared."

"I miss you too, Anna, I'm just trying to get to know Nix better. I like him a lot."

"I know you do," Anna blurted. "It just would've been nice to hang out with you today is all."

"Well, how about we make plans for just the two of us to spend the day together?" I asked, hoping to appease both her and my guilty conscience.

"Yes, I would love that. How about next Sunday we do pedis and brunch?"

"Perfect. I can't wait," I said, leaning in to give her a hug. She squeezed me tight, and hung on for a little longer than I was comfortable with. "Good night, babe."

Chapter 13

Phoenix

I went into work the next day with a smile on my face, which was fairly uncommon for me. Charlie immediately noticed.

"What's going on with you?" he asked me as soon as I walked in.

"Not much," I said in my usual short manner.

"Well, you rarely come in grinning. Are things going well with Lauren?"

"Yes."

"God, getting info out of you is like pulling teeth," he said, exasperated.

I chuckled and hit him on the shoulder before putting my belongings in my locker and getting my gear on. A call came in as soon as I was changed and we headed out. I could tell it was going to be a busy day.

Call after call came in. We went to each one and dealt with them as quickly as possible before heading back out. We didn't even have time for lunch. Then at the very end of the day, just as things were slowing down, we got one more call. There was a lady out on a ledge. She had a bottle of liquor in her hand, and was screaming and crying loudly. We rushed over since we were right down the street. Charlie and I quickly ran up the steps as fast as we could while they tried to coax her down from below with a megaphone.

Upon getting to the floor, we saw the open window, and just as I got to it, she threw the bottle down at the firefighters below, and spread her arms like she was going to fall forward. Before my brain had even caught up with me, I reached out and snagged one of her hands. I tried to pull her into the building, but she fought against me, and soon she was dangling from my fingertips over the ledge, still struggling.

"Let me go, you fucking prick!" she screamed at me.

"Charlie, help me out, man!" I yelled at him.

He squeezed through the window with me and grabbed her arm right underneath where I held her. Between the two of us, we were able to hoist her into the building. I got her underneath me, and put all of my weight on top of her to keep her from doing something stupid.

She looked up at me, her eyes filled with hatred. "I won't ever forget you, you motherfucker," she seethed.

"I bet you will—tomorrow when you're sober," I said back to her, not concerned in the least.

"Not likely, Mr. Narrow," she sneered, glancing down at my name printed on my uniform before spitting into my face. "I didn't want to be saved, you asshole. I've done something so horrible, I can't live with myself anymore!" she shrieked.

"Well, you can get help, ma'am. There are other options for you out there," Charlie offered.

"Not for me," she said, staring at him before breaking down into sobs beneath me.

Just then, the cops came up, put her in handcuffs, and led her off.

"Hey, see if the EMTs downstairs can give her a sedative or something. She needs to be unconscious while she sleeps this shit off," I told them, feeling sorry for her.

That night, I got home and had the realization that life was short.

I shouldn't be spending it doing something I wasn't crazy about. I decided to take Lauren's advice and look at Etsy. After skimming through the site, and doing some research on how much pieces like mine were selling, I decided to open up my own account.

I started by putting only three things on there for sale, but hey, it was a start. Life was short. No time like the present.

That Saturday, I had the day off, and I decided to work on some new projects for the site. I started on an end table in a dark mahogany wood, simple but beautiful. I worked for a few hours before heading inside to make lunch.

I decided to check my account and see if I had any views. As soon as I opened it, I was floored to find out that all three of my pieces had sold. I was so shocked that I stared at the screen for a full five minutes. I then looked at my PayPal just to double-check that what I was seeing was real. Sure enough, it was. I rushed to text Lauren.

Hey, sweetness. I've got some good news.

Well, what is it? she immediately texted back.

You'll have to come over to find out.

I'm at work right now, but I'll be done at seven and I'll head over after!

Five hours. That was perfect. I could do some more work on the table and then clean up before she arrived.

Perfect. See you then.

I quickly finished my lunch and went back out to my shop to keep working. Seeing the sales had lit a fire under my ass, one that I was very grateful for.

Four hours later, I had everything assembled, the only thing left to do was sand it and stain it. I should've stopped an hour earlier, but I was so close to having it done that I had to see it through.

I quickly cleaned up my shop and made my way inside for a shower. When I came out, I realized that my house wasn't the cleanest, and I scrambled to get it at least somewhat put together before Lauren arrived.

At 7:30, there was a knock on the door. Feeling suddenly nervous, I ran my hands over my shirt, smoothing it as much as I could before letting her in.

"Hey, handsome," she said in greeting, leaning in for a kiss.

"Hey, sweetness. Come on in," I replied after pressing my lips to hers.

Once she stepped inside, I realized that she was holding a bottle of champagne and a bag of to-go food.

"I figured I'd bring champagne for the good news, even though I don't know what it is yet. I also picked up some Chinese food. I hope you like lo mein and sesame chicken."

"I love both. Thanks for picking those up."

"So what's the good news?" she asked.

"I sold some pieces on Etsy," I told her.

"You did? I didn't even know you were going to do that. That's amazing!" she exclaimed.

"I came home from a rough day at work on Monday and I decided that life was too short. Fuck it."

"Well, this definitely calls for champagne. I'm glad I stopped," she said, ripping the foil from the bottle.

"I don't have anything fancy to put that in," I told her.

"Fuck that. We don't need glasses. We're drinking straight from the bottle, baby," she said, smiling.

She popped the cork and soon we were toasting.

"To following your dreams," she said, thrusting the bottle into the air before taking a big swig and handing it off to me. I followed suit before leaning in to give her an open-mouthed kiss. She wrapped her arms around my neck, giggling into my mouth. She broke away a moment later. "Okay, before this gets any steamier, I need to eat."

"Yeah, you'll need it to keep your energy up," I growled in her ear, smacking her on the ass.

"Don't tease," she said, looking hopefully into my eyes.

"Not teasing, sweetness. I'm going to ravage you tonight."

"Well, we better eat quickly then."

In no time at all, we had put a decent dent in the food and were putting away the leftovers. When we were finished I came up behind her and trapped her against the counter. I put both of my hands on top of hers and dragged my teeth along her neck as I ground my growing erection against her ass. She hummed deep in her throat as she tipped her head to the side, giving me better access.

"Let's go to bed," I whispered in her ear.

"I'll grab the champagne," she breathed, running off to grab the bottle, and taking a big swig before handing it to me. I took a drink before giving it back to her and picking her up and carrying her to my bedroom.

"Don't drink too much of this. I don't want a repeat of last time. I want you to be a hundred percent sure that you want this," I told her, staring into her eyes as I set her gently on the bed.

"I am one hundred and ten percent sure, Phoenix. And I'm so sorry about last time. It was just so new, and you are the first man I've even looked at since Ryan. I felt guilty. Now I've accepted that he's gone and that I'm allowed to be with someone else. I've moved on to a new phase in my life. It just took me a minute to be comfortable with it," she said, her eyes slightly misty, but full of certainty and conviction.

I didn't reply out loud. There were no words that felt right, so I showed her instead. I stroked her cheek with my thumb, catching a stray tear, before lowering my mouth to hers. I poured everything I felt for her into that kiss, drowning her in my intensity, but she gave just as good as she got, her tongue wrestling for dominance. I let her think she was in control for a moment, but took over, grasping her hair as I bit down on her lip. She instantly relinquished control as she moaned enthusiastically into my mouth. In that instant, I knew that she was the perfect woman for me, but the time for dominance would come. Now, I wanted to absolutely worship her.

My hands made their way to the hem of her shirt, and slowly inched it up her body, goosebumps appearing in their wake. When her breasts were exposed, I discovered she was wearing a black lace bra that left very little to the imagination, and I hummed in appreciation. My head dipped to latch on to her nipple through the fabric. It quickly hardened underneath my attention. I switched to her opposite breast and gave it equal treatment. I reached for the band of her pants, and tugged them impatiently down her legs. When she was an incoherent mess, I licked my way down her torso, dipping my tongue into her belly button before continuing downward. Her panties matched her bra, and I took a moment to appreciate the view of her lying there in her lingerie, spread out before me to do whatever I wanted with. Soon I was peeling both off her, throwing them off to the side. I swiped my tongue through her slit once before lying next to her on my back.

"Phoenix? Why'd you stop?" she asked, confused.

"Sit on my face, Lauren. I want your juices coating me." She didn't move, just stared at me. "I wasn't asking. Sit. On. My. Face."

She looked at me hesitantly for a moment, self-consciousness taking over her features before she moved to straddle my head. I could already smell her essence permeating the air, and my mouth watered.

She slowly lowered herself down on top of my mouth, unsure at first. I immediately latched my lips around her clit, encouraged by the sounds coming out of her. I wrapped my arms around her hips and forced her to move on top of me. She was a little awkward, uncomfortable with having herself bared to me so intimately, but the more I moved my tongue, the more she let go of her insecurities.

Soon, she was riding my face freely, and watching her give in was the most beautiful thing. No longer needing to help her move, my hands roamed up toward her breasts, squeezing them and feeling their fullness. Her hands moved to cover my own as she looked down and locked eyes with me. It was an incredibly intimate moment, and I could tell she felt it too. My fingers began pinching and rolling her nipples, and she became more erratic, grinding into my face harder, her moans becoming louder and louder.

"Phoenix, I'm going to come!" she cried.

I pulled both of her nipples, hard, and gently bit down on her clit at the same time. She immediately detonated, falling forward as she pulsed around my tongue. I lapped up her orgasm, groaning at the taste of her, salty and sweet. She looked down at me, smiling shyly.

"That was so sexy, Lauren," I told her as she climbed off of me. She leaned down and plunged her tongue into my mouth before sucking my lip hard.

"Mmm. I taste good," she said, her voice rough from her orgasm.

"Oh, fuck. You really are the perfect woman for me."

"I know. Now it's my turn," she growled, pulling my pants down. As soon as my cock sprang free, I heard her sharp inhale. "Jesus, you're huge."

"Well, it's not the first time you've had contact with it," I said, chuckling, secretly loving the praise.

"True, but I was very drunk and it's been a few months." She dragged her digit along my length before grasping me fully in her hand and rubbing her thumb around the head, paying special attention to my Prince Albert piercing. "God, this is so sexy. I've never been with a guy who had this before. Does it feel good?" Her voice was becoming more rough by the second.

"Oh, fuck yes it does. Especially when you touch it," I groaned loudly as a bead of precum came out of the tip. She caught it with her thumb before bringing it to her mouth and sucking. She locked eyes with me, moaning as the flavor hit her tongue. I growled at the sight, grabbed her neck, and slammed her lips to mine. She continued to stroke me up and down before breaking away from the kiss and lowering her head to join her hand.

The first touch of her wet, warm mouth wrapping around my length nearly had me coming down her throat, but I somehow held back, delighting in the exquisite torture. My fingers tangled in her hair, unconsciously guiding her rhythm. She pulled back several times to twirl her tongue around my piercing before sucking it and then diving back in. After a few minutes of this, I couldn't stand it anymore. I gripped her hair close to her roots before pulling her hard up toward me. In that moment, all I could think of was kissing her, showing her how much she already meant to me.

I broke away when we were both breathless. "I want you so bad, sweetness," I told her, not disguising the need in my voice.

"Me too, Phoenix. I need you inside me."

"Are you sure this time? We can wait if you need to," I told her, not wanting to rush her into something she wasn't ready for.

"Phoenix, would you just fuck me already?" she asked, exasperated, making me chuckle. I quickly moved my fingers to her entrance, seeing if she was ready for me.

"Fuck, sweetness. You're gushing for me."

She gripped my cock again, brought it to her pussy, and swiped it through her folds. We both moaned at the contact.

I quickly grabbed both her hands, pinning her to the mattress. I decided to tease her just a bit more. I brought my mouth to her ear, laving it and sucking it into my mouth before slowly moving down her body. I stopped at her neck, softly biting it and licking away the hurt. By the time I got to my target, her nipples, she was an incoherent mess, trying and failing to grind her lower body against mine.

"Phoenix, please!" she begged.

I ignored her as I continued to torture her. I switched between her beautiful tits, her nipples erect and straining toward my face. When she was writhing beneath me, I ground my erection against her slick cunt. She coated me instantly, making me lose my composure just a bit.

After another couple of minutes, I decided to put us both out of our misery. I grabbed myself in hand and guided the head to her entrance. I pulled back just a fraction so that I could look into her eyes as I entered her.

I pushed in just a fraction of an inch, watching the pleasure take over her features, before thrusting hard into her wet heat. I immediately brought my mouth to hers, our pleasurable noises intermingling until we couldn't tell who was making what sound.

I pulled back slowly before powerfully surging into her again. I felt as if I was about to lose my head, which I didn't like to do. I liked to take my time, driving her wild and bringing her to climax several times before I lost control. Lauren fucked with my mind in the best possible way, but it screwed up my plan just a bit.

"Sweetness, tell me how you're feeling," I commanded her, wanting her to talk dirty to me.

"God, so good, Phoenix."

"No, tell me the sensations in your body. In detail. I want to hear all of it. I want to hear the dirty, sordid thoughts you're having and every nasty word drip from your mouth."

"I can't. It's too much," she said, moaning.

Even though it almost killed me, I stopped moving inside her. "I won't start moving again until you tell me."

"Phoenix, please," she begged, attempting to move underneath me. I stilled her movements and she groaned in frustration. "Okay." She groaned. "I feel like I'm on fire, in the best possible way," she started, and I rewarded her by pushing myself as deep as I could inside her. "I feel so full that I could overflow and explode." I growled as she kept talking, encouraging her. I could see the fire in her eyes, could tell that while she was hesitant at first, she loved talking to me like this. "My pussy is so wet that I can feel it dripping down to my ass and coating your sheets. Your dick is pulsing inside me each time I contract around you and it makes me want you to be there forever, filling me continually over and over again." At this point, we were both getting very excited, and our breathing was almost bordering on hyperventilating.

"Fuck, Lauren. I'm so hard for you. You're making me lose my fucking mind. I can't think straight when I'm inside you," I groaned against her neck as I felt her legs wrap around me and squeeze, the new position forcing me even deeper inside of her. "Shit, baby. I need you to come again. I want to feel you leaking all over me. I want there to be a puddle underneath you from how hard I make you come." I moved my thumb to her clit, rubbing furiously to get her to climax before me. Within seconds, she was screaming out my name and writhing underneath me. The contractions of her pussy on my cock sent me over the edge, and I spilled myself inside of her.

When I pulled out of her minutes later, I noticed something. Something bad.

"Fuck. I forgot a condom," I said, swearing under my breath.

"It's okay. I'm on birth control, and I'm clean," she told me, smiling.

"Oh, good. I'm clean too," I told her. "Just a second, I'll be right back." I went into the bathroom to wet a washcloth, which I brought back to clean her up. She went to take it from me, but I batted her hands away, wanting to look after her myself. I looked up at her to find her red with embarrassment, but with a warm smile on her face.

After I was finished, I climbed into bed next to her, and pulled her tightly against me, her back to my chest. "Promise you'll be here when I wake up?" I asked her.

"I promise," she said, already dozing off next to me.

Chapter 14

Lauren

I woke up the next morning wrapped around Phoenix like a vine. Besides the night we had both been trashed, it was the first time I'd slept next to a man since Ryan passed. I had forgotten how much I missed it. There was something about sleeping next to someone else that was so comforting. Like you weren't alone in the world anymore.

I sighed and stretched my arms above my head, delighting in the sated feeling deep in my bones. It was the sign of a very good night's sleep, free of any nightmares or late-night anxieties.

My bladder screamed at me when I shifted, causing me to reluctantly get out of bed to take care of business. When I was finished, I looked in the mirror, something I rarely did anymore, to find a content-looking woman opposite me. It was a pleasant surprise. Usually when I looked at my reflection, I saw a stranger, exhausted and haunted, which was why it was a rare occurrence for me to do so. That morning, I found a lost part of myself staring back at me.

I came back to the bedroom to find Phoenix stirring. He glanced up at me before taking in my almost-naked body. All I wore was his T-shirt from the night before.

"I could get used to this view," he told me, his voice rough from sleep.

"So could I," I replied, making the same perusal of his naked body, he was covered from the waist down with a white sheet. I could see his erection straining against the sheet, tenting it, and I licked my lips.

"Are you hungry?" he asked me.

"Yes," I answered, my voice hoarse as I stared at him in appreciation.

"Not for me. For breakfast," he said, chuckling. "I'll take care of your other hunger after." My stomach chose that time to growl loudly. "I'll take that as a yes then?"

I nodded before walking out to the kitchen. I opened his fridge to see what we could make. I pulled out eggs as well as biscuits and bacon. Phoenix came out a minute later, wearing only a pair of shorts. I was momentarily distracted. "Now, how am I supposed to cook with you wearing that? I won't be able to concentrate."

"I never asked you to cook, sweetness. I was going to do that," he replied, smacking my ass, hard.

"Ouch!" I cried, taken by surprise. Even more surprising was how much I liked it. I could feel a heat blooming out from where his palm connected to other areas, making me instantly wet.

"You know you liked it," he teased, coming over to rub his hand in soothing circles on my backside, making the heat even more intense, changing it to pure pleasure. I couldn't help but moan. I looked up at Phoenix to see all trace of teasing gone. His eyes were on fire as he grabbed my hips in both hands and pulled my aching core against his manhood, grinding it roughly between our bodies. After about thirty seconds, when we were both groaning and breathless, he broke away. "Fuck, baby. You drive me crazy."

"Why'd you stop?" I asked.

"'Cause I told you, I want to cook you breakfast. Now sit down, wench," he said jokingly in a deep voice. I chuckled as I sat at the breakfast bar, just watching him cook and move around the kitchen.

Fifteen minutes later, he had everything done and we were scarfing down our food. It seemed as though we had worked up quite the appetite from the previous night.

"That was delicious. Thank you," I said when we were both finished, leaning in to give him a kiss. "Can I use your shower?" I asked, wanting to wash off.

"Sure, babe," he said, leading me to the master bath. I was a little too out of it and distracted when I first got up to really appreciate it, but I did now. It was beautiful and huge. He had a walk-in shower with subway tiles everywhere, there was even a bench in it, a huge soaking tub, and his and hers sinks. The floor tiles were black and there were dark wood slabs behind the sinks. There was also a separate little space for the toilet. Needless to say, it was my dream bathroom. Phoenix leaned in to turn the shower on for me, and soon there was steam filling the space.

"Want to join me?" I asked seductively.

"Wet and naked in a hot shower with you? Who could say no?"

We both stripped out of what little clothes we had on and made our way under the warm water. A contented sigh escaped me as it washed over me, and I dipped my head back to get my hair wet. I felt hands wandering my chest and opened my eyes to see Phoenix washing my torso for me, although I doubted it was any hardship to him. He spent extra time on my breasts, tweaking my nipples until they were tight, hard points. He put more lather in his hands and wrapped his arms around me to wash my back. His hands ventured lower, onto my ass, as he kneaded the tight globes of muscle. Soon, I was unconsciously rubbing myself against him as I grabbed on to his shoulders to steady myself. He brought his mouth down on mine, plunging his tongue in between my lips in time with his cock thrusting against me.

He pulled back, looking down at me before quickly spinning me around. "Rinse off, Lauren. I'm taking you to bed. I want to try something with you," he whispered to me as he took my earlobe between his teeth and tugged. I quickly did as he said and stepped out to towel off. When we were both dry, he picked me up and set me gently in the middle of the bed. "Do you trust me?" he asked me seriously, standing above me, looking like a sculpture carved from stone, completely beautiful and erect for me. He looked dominating, intimidating, and gentle all at the same time.

I looked into his eyes, and realized that I absolutely did, which somewhat surprised me, considering I hardly knew him. "Yes."

He smiled at me for a beat, "Good. Now, there are things I would like to do with you, and from your behavior, I think you'll be receptive to them, but if anything makes you uncomfortable, you need to tell me immediately."

"Phoenix, what's going on? You're making me a little nervous."

"You don't need to be nervous, sweetness." The use of his nickname for me settled my anxiety somewhat, and I gave him a tight smile in encouragement. "I have a bit of a dominant personality, and I like to explore that in the bedroom," he said before grabbing some black silk sashes from beside the bed. I glanced at them before looking into his questioning eyes. I swallowed hard and realized that the thought of him dominating me in bed made me nervous but intensely turned on. "I want to tie you up and blindfold you. I want to have you laid out before me, completely at my mercy. I want to torture you with pleasure, using my hands and mouth and cock all over you until you are begging me. What do you think, sweetness? Are you willing?"

I got wetter and wetter with each word that came out of his mouth, and I could feel myself dripping onto the sheets underneath me. My mouth was dry as I responded, "Yes."

He looked relieved and fire immediately came to life behind his eyes. "Good. Now, you don't need a safe word. If something makes you uncomfortable, just tell me and I'll stop." At my nod, he turned fully into a dom right before my eyes. While I was incredibly nervous, I felt like I had never been this turned on in my life.

"Arms and legs spread out wide." I did as he said, and he went to work restraining all of my limbs, tying each one to a different point on his bed. When I was completely immobilized, he looked down at me with a gentle look in his eyes. "God, you look so fucking hot. I've wanted you like this since I first laid eyes on you. Feeling okay so far?"

"Yes," I said, my voice rough.

"Be specific with me. How does it make you feel?" he asked, trailing his fingers down slowly over my bound body. Once he reached my pussy, he dragged a fingertip through my wetness, no doubt knowing exactly how it was making me feel.

"It makes me feel nervous but excited at the same time. No one has ever done this to me before."

"Well, your body is telling me that you like this a lot." He pulled his finger from my folds and held it to my mouth, painting my lips with my essence. "Suck," he commanded.

I did as I was told, sucking every bit of my wetness from him and moaning as the flavor hit my tongue. I didn't expect to like it, but I did, maybe because of how dirty I felt doing it.

Phoenix turned and grabbed something from the nightstand. Before I could ask or see what it was, he had it over my eyes. A blindfold then, I thought. He didn't touch me or make a sound after that, for what felt like forever, but in reality was probably only a minute. Everything was heightened; my ears strained to hear any sound at all, but only my heavy breathing filled the room. My skin almost burned with the anticipation of being touched. I could smell my arousal strong in the air, as well as still taste it on my tongue.

"Phoenix, please," I begged, for what I didn't know.

"Hush, sweetness. I'll take care of you," he whispered in my ear, his breath causing goosebumps to rise on my overly heated skin.

He started planting kisses along my jawline before dragging his lips down my body, all over my torso, except the places I wanted it most. He explored every inch of me except for my breasts. His mouth was the only thing touching me, and I strained toward him, searching for more contact. Finally, after I was a writhing, moaning mess, he latched his lips around a nipple, making me cry out. He laved it for minutes before giving the other one equal attention. When he decided they had enough, he bit down on both before going farther south. I felt relieved, thinking that he would be giving me what I so desperately wanted, but was immediately frustrated when he gave my lower half of my body the same treatment as the top, skirting around everywhere except for my cunt. I pulled against my restraints in vain, as he chuckled against my skin.

"Nix! Lick me already!"

"What do you say, sweetness?" he asked. "Beg me, Lauren."

"Please, Phoenix. I need you. Make me come."

"How do you want me to make you come?"

"Your mouth. Please, your mouth." I didn't even recognize this woman I had become; my voice was unfamiliar, as were the words coming out of me.

Thankfully, he gave me what I wanted. His lips closed around my clit and sucked violently. He groaned, the vibrations traveling through my whole body and intensifying my pleasure. There was no soft buildup because of how much he had teased me beforehand, and I was grateful. I didn't think I could've taken any more delicious torture. He didn't just lick me, he feasted, making a meal out of my flesh. Within minutes, I was crying out my release and bucking against his face.

"Phoenix, I want you inside me," I told him, needing to be filled.

"Come for me again, and then I'll give you whatever you want," he told me, his voice like gravel.

"I want you inside me when I come again," I pleaded with him.

"You will, sweetness, after this orgasm," he said before pushing his fingers into my wetness. I arched off the bed, loving the intrusion. His mouth went back to work on my breasts, licking, sucking, and biting, as his fingers plunged in and out of me quickly. I could already feel myself building again. As restrained as I was, I could still move a little bit and started fucking myself with his hand. He growled his appreciation against my chest. Just when I was about to tumble over the edge, he switched it up, stroking my inner walls as opposed to pulling in and out. I felt a strange sensation, like I had to pee. It was intense and pleasurable, but also slightly uncomfortable. The longer he did it, the stronger the feeling became. I felt the need to push, but didn't want to pee on him, so I held back. When I was an incoherent mess, and thoroughly torn, Phoenix murmured against my chest, "Let go, Lauren. Let it all go."

I reluctantly did as he said, and felt a huge orgasm rip through me. It was unlike anything else I had felt before, and it just kept going and going. I suddenly felt warm wetness underneath me, and was mortified, thinking that I had peed all over him and the bed, before he groaned and said, "Fuck, you're squirting all over me. Give me more. More." He started moving his fingers faster inside me and rubbed over my clit quickly with his other hand, intensifying my orgasm and making more wetness shoot out. I could feel it spraying all over me and the bed. I started screaming, no longer able to control myself.

When it stopped, Phoenix pulled his fingers from me and took my blindfold off. I blinked against the brightness, before looking up into his eyes. They were on fire as he looked down at me, slowly lowering his weight onto me. "You're a naughty girl. You made a mess all over my bed," he scolded me. I started blushing, but before I could apologize, he grabbed my chin and forced my gaze back to his. "That was the sexiest thing I have ever seen. I'm going to make you do that lots, so get used to it."

82

He sat up and reached down to untie my ankles, but left my arms restrained. "We're going to be really dirty now and fuck all over your squirt. Every time you feel that wetness under you, think of how it felt to let it all go," he told me as he plunged into me. We both groaned once he was fully inside of me. "Wrap your legs around me." As soon as I did, he instantly felt deeper. "Hang on, baby, this is going to be quick and rough."

True to his word, he thrust into me over and over, hard and deep. I held on tight with my legs, pulling him even deeper inside me. I could see sweat breaking out across his brow with the exertion. He put one of his hands under my ass, bringing my hips up even farther and using it to pull me against his thrusts. He squeezed me tightly, and I knew there would be bruises from his fingers tomorrow. The thought only excited me more, and I could hear how wet I was.

"I can feel you leaking all over my cock. You feel so good," he told me as he continued ramming into me. "Are you close? I need to feel you coming on me again," he ground out between clenched teeth.

"Yes, Phoenix. Come with me. Now!" I cried, looking into his eyes as I contracted around him. A moment later, I could feel his hot semen squirting inside me, feel his dick pulsing.

He reached up to untie my hands before collapsing on top of me, his body still inside of mine. We lay there in the aftermath for a few minutes before he gave me a kiss and moved his weight off of me.

"How are you?" he asked me, searching my face.

"So good. I had no idea it could be like that."

"Baby, we're just getting started. I took it easy on you today, but it will get more intense each time."

I chuckled before looking down, embarrassment coloring my cheeks again once I saw how wet the bedding was. "I'm sorry I made such a mess. I've never done that before," I told him. Surprise took over his features before he smiled widely.

"Oh, baby. I think you've just made me one of the happiest, cockiest men in the world with that statement. And don't be sorry. That was one of the sexiest things I've ever seen in my life."

After that, we got up and I pulled on my pants but put on one of his shirts instead of mine. I buried my nose in the collar and inhaled deeply. Oh, God. It smelled delicious, like sandalwood, leather, orange, his wood shop, a hint of sweat, and something that was purely Phoenix.

We spent the afternoon just hanging out. It felt comfortable to be here at his house. It felt as though I had known him for years as opposed to months. We cuddled on the couch and turned on TCM, watching old movies for hours.

At three o'clock, I decided to check my phone as I hadn't looked at it since the night before. I had ten missed calls from Anna and five texts.

Hey, lady! You didn't come home last night. Everything okay?

Are we still on for today?

Dude, I thought we were supposed to hang out today.

Lauren, you're freaking me out. ARE YOU OKAY?!

If you aren't dead in a ditch somewhere, I am super fucking pissed at you.

Shit. I had completely forgotten about my plans with her. I called her immediately.

"Hey," she answered, sounding equally relieved and pissed off in the same breath.

"Anna! I'm so sorry! I went to Nix's last night after work and we've been a bit preoccupied today that I haven't even checked my phone," I said, my voice pleading with her to forgive me.

"Whatever, Lauren. Thanks for keeping me updated on where you were going," she snapped.

"I'm so sorry, Anna, really. It's still early. I'll come home and change and we can go out."

"Just forget about it. I can see where I rank on your important scale," she said, and then hung up on me.

Shit.

Chapter 15

Lauren

I walked through the front door of our apartment an hour later to find Anna's bedroom door closed. Fuck. I was hoping that she would be out in the living room so we could talk about everything. I debated if I should knock on her door or not. It really seemed like she wanted to be left alone, but I didn't want to leave things how they were. Finally, I decided to just go for it. Fuck it.

"Anna, come out so we can talk."

"Fuck you, Lauren."

"Come on, Anna. Please. I really don't want to leave things like this between us."

She didn't respond, and just as I was about to give up and go to my room, her door opened.

"Anna, I am so sorry. I really didn't mean to forget. I didn't even think I would be spending the night there, but I went over after work and then one thing led to another and…" I trailed off, not really knowing what else to say.

"Yeah, you said all of that on the phone." She looked at me with her eyebrows raised, waiting for me to continue. When I stayed silent, she started in. "You know, it was your idea to hang out today, and then you just don't even show up or bother answering any of my texts or calls."

"I know, Anna, I wish I could do something to change it, but I can't. Just please understand that I didn't do any of this on purpose. I would never intentionally do something like this."

"I know you wouldn't, but Jesus, Lauren. You didn't even bother telling me that you weren't coming home last night. I was worried," she snapped. She just kept lecturing me no matter what I said. It was starting to piss me off a bit.

"You know, I don't have to tell you everything just because we're roommates," I snapped back, sick of apologizing and taking her shit.

She looked at me like I had slapped her. "Are you fucking kidding me? I wasn't aware that being concerned about your safety made me a shitty friend."

"Well, you're not my mother, Anna. I get we live together, but I'm a fucking adult, and I can do what I want. Not to mention the fact that I have been holed up in this apartment with you for so long. I finally have a desire to go out and be with people, to socialize…"

"So, suddenly I'm not people? Being with me isn't socializing? I'm just the 'friend' that you don't want to be around anymore?"

"Anna, you know I didn't mean it like that. I love hanging out with you, but I pretty much only hang out with you, especially since Savannah is busy with Charlie. I meant doing something different with my life than sitting on the couch, drinking wine, and mourning the life I lost. I get that you're pissed about today, but can't you just get over it and say, 'I'm happy for you, Lauren. I'm happy that you are finding some shred of happiness after everything that happened to you. You deserve that'?"

"I *am* happy that you're finding all of that stuff, but you don't have to completely forget about the friends you have now. The ones who dragged you through that rough patch. Who helped put you back together after he died. I did that. I was here for you. Not Phoenix. And now you're treating me like I don't even exist on your radar anymore. Like I served my purpose, and now I'm being tossed away like a dirty cum rag."

"It wasn't *you* who put me back together after he died, it was *me*! I appreciate you being there for me and for giving me a place to stay and helping me out of my rut, but ultimately I am the one who came out of that on the other side. You have no idea what it's like to lose someone so important to you like that!" I screamed at her.

"You have no fucking clue what I've been through, so don't preach to me! I've been through more shit than you can ever imagine!" she yelled at me, tears streaming down her face. With that, she slammed her door in my face, leaving me to feel like the biggest asshole in the world.

———— ⦿⦿ ————

The next day, I went into work to find that it was super slow. There were a bunch of us just sitting around not doing anything. It was not good for me. I was hoping that I would come in and the salon would be extremely busy so that work would take my mind off of everything. Instead, I was sitting in my stylist chair, staring at my message thread with Anna. I couldn't find the right words to say to her. I felt so awful. I had no idea that she had felt that way.

With a sigh, I locked my phone and set it in my lap. I looked down at my left hand, finding my engagement ring still firmly on my ring finger. I played with it for a moment, thinking about how different my life had been when this was first placed on my hand. It was a constant reminder of Ryan, which I liked sometimes, but I think it was holding me back still.

My decision made, I slowly slid it off my finger. All my breath came out of my body with a *whoosh*. I could feel a few tears slipping down my face, but I batted them away. I took off my necklace to put the ring on the chain before clasping it back around my neck. I immediately felt a weight that I didn't know was even there lift off of me.

"Veronica!" I called to my fellow stylist, the one who had actually given me Savannah's information that first time I wanted to get a tattoo.

"What's up?" she asked.

"Want to color my hair?"

"Yes! Jesus, it's about time, girl. I hate this color on you," she said bluntly.

"Tell me how you really feel," I teased her, laughing.

"Well, it's true. It's not a bad color, it's just too plain for you."

We quickly discussed what I wanted and she got to work. Maybe it wouldn't be such a bad thing that today was slow after all. I was finally officially moving on with my life and starting a new chapter.

When she finished rinsing the color out and blow drying my hair, she slowly turned my chair around to face the mirror. I sucked in a breath, not able to stop staring at the woman looking back at me. It was me again. Not the same me as before, but I had finally gotten this part of myself back.

I hadn't gone nearly as colorful as I used to, and I was glad I went that route. It felt more like the current me. We had done a medium brown all over with pink highlights that were pulled into a kind of balayage at the ends. She had also given me a cut, nothing too crazy, just a trim and some layers, giving my hair a bit more dimension.

"Well?" she asked.

"I love it," I told her, slightly teary-eyed. "Thank you so much." I got up to give her a big hug. She was slightly surprised at first, because I rarely touched anyone anymore, but she got over it quickly and hugged me back tightly in response.

As soon as I was done with that, I texted Savannah.

Hey, lady. Can you fit me in for a tattoo?

Of course, babe! When?

ASAP.

Is today too soon?

Hell no. This has been long overdue. I'll be there at 4.

See you then!

I pulled up to the shop at 3:55 and headed inside. Upon seeing me, Savannah squealed.

"Holy shit, girl! You look fantastic!"

"Thanks, lady," I told her, giving her a tight hug. "Thank you for getting me in on such short notice."

"Of course. I figured you might want to do something for them when you were ready. That's what this is, right?"

"Yeah. It's time."

"So, what are you thinking?"

"I want the words *We only part to meet again* with a bird and then a really small bird flying off," I told her, becoming slightly teary.

"It's beautiful, Lauren. A wonderful way to honor them," she said, leaning in to give me a hug. I pulled back before I started full-on crying. After we picked a font, she got everything prepared and printed off the stencil.

"Where do you want it?"

"Right underneath my collarbone, leading up to my shoulder."

She put the stencil on, I lay back on her table, and we got started. Once we settled in, we started chatting.

"So, I haven't seen you in a while. How are things going? Anything new?" she asked.

"Well, I started dating Phoenix," I said quietly.

"It's about damn time, bitch!" she said excitedly, making me chuckle.

"Yeah, I know. It took me a while, but things are going really well."

"That's awesome! I'm so happy for you. If anyone deserves happiness, it's you."

"Thanks, Savannah."

"So, anything else? I know about the yoga classes. How are things with you and Anna? Still like living together?" I swallowed and looked away, avoiding her questioning gaze. "Uh-oh. That doesn't look good. What happened?" she asked me. She was entirely too perceptive.

"We had a fight. It kind of started last weekend. She feels like I'm not spending any time with her anymore, and I was going to make it up to her yesterday, but I spent the night with Nix and I totally spaced. When I finally got around to checking my phone, she had blown it up and was super pissed and worried. I got home and we started yelling at each other and now we're not talking," I rushed, trying to get it all out.

"That blows. So, what now?"

"I'm not sure. I feel like such a bitch. I want to make it up to her somehow, but I don't really know how to go about it. Have any ideas?" I asked.

"Maybe you can plan a day together. I bet she would really like that."

"Well, that's what yesterday was supposed to be. She won't even come out of her room. I doubt she would agree to go or do anything with me right now."

"Hmm. Maybe you can get her something? And put a little 'I'm sorry' note with it?"

"Yeah, that's a good idea. What should I get her?" I asked.

"Bitch, I'm not coming up with everything for you. Besides, you're her roommate. You know her way better than I do."

"Oh, fine," I said, rolling my eyes.

She finished my tattoo and I gave her a hug before leaving. She insisted on not charging me, telling me that she knew I was going to get something for them and had always planned on doing it for free.

I climbed into my car, texting Phoenix to see if I could come over. I had an idea about how to smooth things over with Anna, but I needed his help.

Chapter 16

Phoenix

I had just stepped out of the shower when Lauren texted me about coming over. I quickly responded BTB—Bring That Booty. She sent me back a Darryl gif, clearly getting my *Office* reference.

I got dressed and went downstairs to get some drinks ready for when she arrived. I poured a glass of red wine for her, knowing it was her favorite, and took a beer out of the fridge for myself.

Five minutes later, my doorbell rang, and I brought her wine to the door as I opened it. She stepped into the light and my breath caught in my throat.

"Hi," she said nervously.

"Hey, sweetness. You look absolutely gorgeous. When did you do this?" I asked.

She looked slightly relieved as she answered. "Thanks, handsome. I did it today at work. I also just came from Savannah's shop, she gave me a new tattoo," she said, pulling her top to the side so I could see the new ink. It also drew my attention to the fact that her engagement ring was now around her neck as opposed to on her finger, and my heart clenched. I dragged my finger from her sternum up to the ring, touching it briefly, making her inhale sharply. My hand continued its journey underneath her tattoo as I admired it.

"It's beautiful, Lauren."

"Thank you," she said breathlessly. I handed her the wine and she took a generous drink as she came in and set her stuff down.

"So, what made you want to do all of this stuff today?"

"I just felt ready for it. All at once. One minute I was looking down at my hand with the ring on it and suddenly I was taking it off. After that it was like a tidal wave. Like I just wanted to start a new chapter, and it all felt right."

Knowing that words wouldn't be enough, I leaned in and kissed her in response. When she moaned into my mouth, I couldn't help but grab her hair by the roots before pulling her to me more tightly. She broke away a moment later, giving me a heated look.

"Want to watch a movie with me?" I asked her, wanting to do something normal and domestic with her.

"Yes," she said simply with a smile on her face.

We sat on my couch as we turned on *Date Night*, eating leftover Mexican food and cuddling up to each other. It felt so normal. Like we were an ordinary couple who had done this a hundred times. I smiled to myself, feeling deeply content. Like we were always meant to be here. When the movie ended, she turned to me with a question in her eyes.

"I have a favor to ask of you."

"What is it, sweetness?"

"Can you make a little jewelry box? Anna and I got into a huge fight last night, and I want to make it up to her."

"Of course, babe. What was the fight about?" I asked, feeling like I already knew.

"You. Us. Me. She basically feels neglected, like I don't care anymore. She's right, of course. I've been a shitty friend, but not on purpose. I've just been distracted, and I've been trying to figure my shit out and start a new chapter."

"You shouldn't feel bad about that, Lauren. Yes, you should make some more time for her, but never feel guilty for trying to give yourself a better life and trying to get over the shit that's happened to you," I told her, looking into her eyes. I understood Anna's feelings, but she shouldn't be mad at Lauren for bettering herself. I briefly wondered if it was something deeper than she was telling her, but I kept my thoughts to myself. "But, to answer your question, yes. I can absolutely do that for you. What do you want it to look like?" I asked.

"Nothing crazy or elaborate. Just a small dark wooden jewelry box with maybe a pretty design on the top. I was thinking I could fill it with fancy jewelry for her piercings." My mind was already spinning with ideas.

"I'll start on it tomorrow, sweetness."

"Oh, thank you!" she exclaimed, giving me a kiss to show her gratitude.

Before things could get heated, she broke away. "I should probably head home," she said with regret.

"Oh," I said, disappointed. "I thought that maybe you would spend the night again."

"I would love to, but I'm thinking I should probably stay at home for the next few days. I don't want to give Anna any more reason to be mad at me."

"Yeah, I get that. Okay," I said, getting up to walk her to the door. "I see the real reason you came over tonight. You just want these magic hands of mine to make something pretty for you," I teased her.

"You can do more than just make pretty things with those magic hands."

I chuckled, kissing her good-night.

———————— ☾☉ ————————

The next day, I started on Anna's box. All Lauren had told me she wanted was a small dark wooden box. I could work with that. It wouldn't take me too long either. Before I started, I made myself breakfast and some coffee, knowing that I would be out there for a few hours working. I decided on steak and eggs. I didn't make it very often because the steak usually took a while, but today I felt like being in the kitchen. I loved cooking. It was one of my passions. It was fun to be able to put a bunch of stuff together and see how it came out. I was especially obsessed with seasonings. You could cook the exact same thing, and it would taste different every time just because of what you seasoned it with. I cooked my steak medium rare, made some over-easy eggs, and sautéed some mushrooms and peppers to have with it.

While I was eating, I also looked at some pictures online just to get an idea of what I liked and what might look good. When I was finished, I headed out to my shop, which was actually in my garage.

Upon walking in, I took a moment to appreciate my space. This was my favorite spot in the house. It was where I could spend hours, just working and not thinking. It took away my anxiety and made me feel calm, collected, and in control. It smelled like all different types of wood and stain. I kept it very neat, not liking clutter, especially in this space, and had all my tools organized and hanging on the wall for me to see.

For Anna's box, I decided to use a dark walnut. Simple, but beautiful. I cut out the pieces that I would need, letting the wood talk to me. You had to work with the wood, not the other way around, something a lot of people didn't realize. The grain already had its grooves and shape to it, so when you worked with it, you had to feel which direction and shape it was pulling you.

After fiddling with it for about three hours, I had a box. It was rectangular in shape, with curved corners. I had also put some grooves in the sides, going all around the box. I knew I was also going to do a design or a carving on the top of it as well, but I needed lunch first.

I quickly dusted myself off so I wouldn't track sawdust all over the house, and washed my hands before looking in my fridge. I pulled out a beer, along with some potato chips and French onion dip. I started snacking on that while I debated on what to make. Pulling out a bunch of sandwich stuff, I figured I didn't need to make a super elaborate lunch considering I had a really decent breakfast. I did, however, pull out all the stops. I had roast beef and turkey, adding all the fixings to it.

I had turned on *The Office* while I was eating, figuring I would take a little bit of a break before I started back in on the box. I put on my favorite episode, "The Dinner Party," and dug into my lunch. Even though I had eaten just a few hours before, I was starving. Woodworking always made me famished, but it still surprised me.

After watching three episodes and finishing two beers, I went back out to sand the box and work on the design. Once it was smooth, I took out my carving tools and got to work on the top. I didn't know Anna super well, but I did know that she enjoyed going to yoga with Lauren, so I figured I would carve an ohm symbol in the middle, with a sun and crescent moon on either side. The carving would probably be the most time consuming part of making this box. I would probably only get the ohm done that day and have to do the sun and moon on a different day.

I finished for the day about two hours later. I quickly took a shower and dressed in some sweats, wanting something comfortable after how much I worked in the shop. I texted Lauren as soon as I was decent.

I've got a big chunk of the box done.

Already? Wow, you must really like me. ;)

Well, I don't work this hard for just anybody.

Can I see a picture?

I smiled to myself at her text, an idea popping into my head. I was going to make her wait and tease her with it for a bit.

Not until it's done.

Aww, really?! What if I say please...?

Nice try, sweetness.

Please...sir?

Oh, God. She had to pull that title out, no doubt having a much better idea why I liked it so much now after the last time we were in bed together.

I said no, Lauren. Now be a good girl and stop begging.

I can be a good girl...

It's still not going to work. I'll text you when it's done so you can come pick it up. And maybe show me how much you appreciate all my hard work.

Oh, I do appreciate it, sir.

I smiled to myself, hard from our banter, and lay on the couch watching TV until I was tired enough for bed.

Chapter 17

Lauren

The next few days in the apartment were tense to say the least. Anna didn't speak a word to me, and whenever I came out into the common area, she immediately went into her room. Needless to say, I was very excited when Phoenix finally texted me to tell me that the box was finished. I had already bought lots of jewelry to fill it with—some cheap stuff, and then a few really beautiful pieces. There was one for a belly button piercing that looked like an opal moon, a simple rose gold septum piece with a hoop and then a triangle that came down underneath, and a gorgeous set of star studs for her ears.

I decided to fit in a quick yoga session before heading over to Nix's place that evening. When I got up to our little yoga loft, I saw that Anna was already using it. I debated just leaving, but I really wanted to practice, and I wouldn't let her make me feel like I was constantly walking on eggshells in my own home.

I went up to my mat, which was already laid out, and started to flow. She looked at me only once when I first walked in, but then went back to her own session. We stood there, each doing our own thing, flowing differently, but almost feeding off of each other, like we were doing a separate dance that complemented each other. I felt the music she'd put on surround me and vibrate through me. Our breathing was like an ocean's waves, washing over us and intermingling with each other's, and the room soon became hot with our body temperatures rising.

Just when I thought that we'd be able to work through our shit without even having to say anything, she suddenly grabbed her water bottle and towel and stormed out of the loft. She clearly hadn't finished her session and was pissed that I had interrupted it.

"Anna, wait! I'll leave, you finish. I'm sorry. I didn't think that would upset you so much," I said, not wanting to piss her off more.

"Yeah, you know what, Lauren? That's your whole problem. You don't think about anyone besides yourself. You don't care that I was there having my own time and space to sort out my shit. You just want to do whatever you want and fuck everyone else," she yelled at me before taking off and slamming her door. I blinked, not even able to process what the fuck had just happened.

I left the space, no longer in the mood to finish my session, let alone be in this apartment anymore. I quickly showered and changed before heading to Nix's. The sooner I got things fixed between us, the better.

I showed up to his house half an hour later. We spent the afternoon eating, talking, and laughing. It surprised me how comfortable I felt with not only him, but with spending so much time in his house. It felt like a safe space for me already, maybe because of all the drama with Anna, but I think I would've felt like that either way.

After lunch, he took me into his shop. I had never been in it before, and it was pretty cool to see the area where he designed and built all of these gorgeous things. It smelled like wood and sweat, with a hint of chemicals, probably from the stain. He kept it immaculate, not a tool out of place, the floor clean, which I could only imagine would be difficult with sawdust.

"Are you ready to see the box?" he asked me.

"Of course," I replied.

He pulled it out from behind his back, and placed it in my palms before stepping back to let me fully admire it. It was phenomenal. Even more beautiful than I had pictured in my head. It was just small enough to fit in both of my hands, the dark wood sanded and stained perfectly, I could still smell it. The design on the top was what really made it unique though. A sun, crescent moon, and an ohm all with lots of swirls to tie them all together. I opened it to find a few pieces of wood inside forming sections. Underneath the lid was the inscription, "You are my person."

"How did you know about this?" I asked him, running my fingertips over the letters.

"I remember you telling me that you and Anna loved watching *Grey's Anatomy* together so I looked up special quotes from the show. That seemed like a suitable one," he said, smiling down at me.

"I can't believe you did all this," I breathed, stunned that he put this much work into it.

"Well, you asked me to," he said simply.

"I know, but I didn't think that you would do this beautiful carving and research stuff to put an engraving on it. It's so special."

"So you like it?" he asked.

"Yes. I love it. It's perfect. Thank you, Phoenix," I told him, leaning in to kiss him.

"You're welcome, sweetness."

"I think it's time to show you how much I appreciate it," I whispered seductively.

"I want to do another scene with you," he growled in my ear. "Would you be down to play a little?" he asked, making wetness immediately flood to my opening.

"Yes, please."

"What I have in mind is quite a bit more intense than last time. Make sure to tell me if you get uncomfortable at all, okay?" I nodded at his words as he grabbed my hand and pulled me inside and toward a door that I had never noticed before.

"Where are we going?" I asked, slightly nervous.

"The basement. I have some equipment set up down there so it's a bit easier."

He opened the door and we went down the stairs. I was expecting something like in *Fifty Shades of Grey*, lots of red, leather, whips and canes everywhere. Something dark and scary, almost like a dungeon, especially since it was in his basement. I was pleasantly surprised though when we got to the bottom of the stairs. It was very warm and bright, and I felt my anxiety lessen. There was plush beige carpet, warm white walls, and exposed brick on the far end. There was also a fur rug in the center of the room with a beautiful sex swing on top of it. The swing was built into a dark wooden frame with support joists on top of it. I immediately wondered if Phoenix had built it.

"I made that about two years ago," he said, answering my unspoken question.

My eyes continued their journey around the room. There were no visible toys anywhere, but there was a huge chest on the wall with the exposed brick, and I would have bet that he had all sorts of stuff in there. There was a plain black bench on one wall as well, along with strange metal hooks and bars along the ceiling. I wasn't quite ready to think about what those might be for yet.

Phoenix, having been paying close attention to me, noticed the direction of my eyes. I immediately felt him behind me, his front to my back, as he whispered in my ear, "Don't worry, sweetness, we won't do anything with those quite yet. I don't think you're ready for that." He chuckled at my exhale of relief. "But you will be soon."

"What are you going to do to me?"

"Well, I was thinking I would bind these beautiful breasts in some rope," he murmured, bringing his hands around to squeeze them through my shirt, making me whimper, "tie your hands behind your back, bend you over the bench there and work your ass over with a riding crop." As much as what he said scared me, it also excited me beyond belief. "Don't worry, I'll go slow and be gentle. I think you're going to love it, but if you don't, just let me know. I want to explore your fantasies and reactions with this. If you're not having fun, then I'm not, okay?" At my nod, he started peeling off my clothes. Despite the warm temperature, goosebumps immediately popped up on my exposed skin.

His lips moved to my neck as he started pulling and tweaking my nipples between his fingertips. I moaned as he gently bit down where my neck and shoulder met. He made quick work of taking my pants and underwear off, leaving me completely naked, and him completely dressed. He then led me over to the bench and pushed at my upper back to get me to bend over. I did, resting my elbows on the bench in front of me, my ass sticking out toward him. He trailed a finger from the back of my neck all the way down my spine, making me shiver. He suddenly pulled his hand back and swatted my ass, leaving a stinging heat behind. I wasn't sure how I felt about it. At first, it hurt and surprised me, but then the sting transformed into a blooming heat, spreading to my pussy. He stroked where he'd hit, before doing the same thing to the other cheek. This time, I moaned, surprising myself.

"Do you like when I spank you, sweetness?" he breathed in my ear. I hummed my approval. He plunged his fingers into my pussy before pulling them out and spreading around my wetness. "Your body is telling me you like it." He spanked me harder this time. "Tell me you like it, Lauren."

"I like it, sir," I moaned, the title slipping out without me realizing.

"Oh, fuck, Lauren. You know what that does to me." He thrust his erection against my ass before pulling away and walking toward the chest. A moment later, he had rope in his hand and he stood me up straight and spun me around. He made quick work of binding my chest, wrapping the rope underneath my breasts and then on top. Lots of tucking and winding of the rope and he had a triangle shape in between them before also sectioning off the outsides. When he was finished, he pulled back to inspect his work, lightly dragging his hands across my chest.

The longer they were in the bind, the more aware I became of them. The rope was bringing more blood to the area, making my nipples pebble further, and then his tongue was lightly swiping both before blowing cool air on them. I moaned and started squirming. I could feel more moisture pooling between my legs and I couldn't stay still.

"Now, your wrists. Ready?" I nodded, turning around and putting both hands behind my back for him. He adjusted the bench higher, and once again gestured for me to lie on it. This time it was high enough that I could comfortably lie facedown on it without support from my hands or arms. He then began to tie my wrists together. "Spread your legs for me." I did as he said, feeling completely exposed to his gaze. "God, you look absolutely stunning like this."

He walked away toward the chest again, and came back with a simple black riding crop. He leaned down to pinch my nipple as he stroked my back with the tip of the crop. The leather felt nice against my skin and I leaned into it. Before I could react, it was pulled away and it landed hard on my ass, the sound echoing loudly through the room. The sting actually wasn't that bad. It sounded bad, but it mostly just felt good. He did it again, and at my moaning, picked up speed. He showered my ass and thighs with the blows, before slowly moving toward my pussy. I tensed in anticipation, and when it finally happened, I almost screamed it was so intense. He struck me multiple times in a row all along the seam of my lips before rubbing the crop through my folds.

"Jesus, you're drenched," he said, his voice low and rough. "Suck." He stuck the riding crop in front of my mouth. I greedily latched on to it, moaning as I tasted myself. Normally, I would be a little ashamed, but he had me so worked up that my flavor only turned me on more. "Are you ready for me to fuck you now?"

"Yes. God, please fuck me. I need you," I begged.

He circled around and stood behind me again, stroking my ass gently with his warm hand. "Your skin is deliciously pink." He knelt down and ran his tongue all over everywhere he'd struck, ending with my pussy. I could feel his whole face buried in between my legs.

"Oh, please," I pleaded loudly.

"Be patient, Lauren," he said sternly, smacking my ass again, only working me up more.

He continued sucking, licking, and plunging his mouth and tongue between my legs until I was a writhing mess. Just when I felt like I was about to come, he pulled back.

"No!" I protested, making him chuckle. "Please, I need to come."

"I'll take care of you, but I want to have some fun first. Delayed gratification makes everything better, sweetness."

He walked back to the chest before returning with a vibrator. He dragged it through my folds, soaking it, before slowly pushing it into me. He turned it on the lowest setting before leaving it inside me. I groaned, frustrated. It was just enough to drive me wild. He came to sit in front of me on the bench.

"Do you want to suck my cock, Lauren?" he asked me, his eyes on fire.

I nodded, locking my gaze with his and licking my lips.

He unzipped his pants and freed his dick, holding it out in front of my face. There was something really sexy about the fact that I was still the only one naked. It almost felt naughtier that way. I gently swiped my tongue up his length and around the head, enjoying his sounds of encouragement. After a few moments, Nix grabbed me roughly by the hair and growled, "Quit teasing." With his hand guiding me, I took him fully into my mouth. It was a little difficult without the use of my hands, but I managed. I sucked him hard, bobbing up and down on him, before taking him to the back of my throat. My eyes watered as I triggered my gag reflex, but I pushed past it, breathing deeply through my nose. "Enough," Nix said, pulling back, also denying himself an orgasm.

"Are you going to finally fuck me?" I asked desperately.

"Not yet," he responded.

He pulled the toy out slowly, turning it on a slightly higher setting before gently pushing it in and out. Just enough to drive me insane but not push me over the edge. He knelt and sucked one of my sensitive nipples into his hot mouth, biting down gently. I felt myself building again, and I ground myself into the bench, trying to get some friction on my clit. He let me for a minute, but as soon as I was about to topple over the edge, he pulled away again.

"Phoenix, please! I can't."

"You can handle it, baby. Just once more and then I'll give you so many orgasms you won't be able to take anymore."

I whimpered as he knelt behind me again and speared me with his tongue. I thrust myself back against him, getting the most I could out of the shallow penetration. I had been so distracted by his tongue that I didn't notice the plug against my asshole until he was slowly pushing it into me. I immediately tensed up, pushing it out, not used to anything back there.

"Relax, sweetness. You'll love it. I promise."

I slowly unclenched as he continued working my pussy with his mouth. When he pushed the tip of the plug in this time, I relaxed against it, letting him in. He slowly fucked me with it until it was fully seated inside of me. I groaned against the sensation, full and filthy, and I felt more wetness drip out of me. By this time, I was sure the bench beneath me was completely slick, but I didn't care. This time, it didn't take me any time to reach my peak, but once again, Nix pulled back. I didn't have much time to be disappointed though, because he was soon filling me with his cock. With the combination of him and the plug, I felt impossibly full and I cried out at the sensation.

He was soon pushing slowly in and out of me, building me higher each time. He also moved the vibrator underneath me to press against my clit. Every thrust pushed the plug in deeper and me harder against the vibrator. Within thirty seconds I was ready to detonate. I whimpered, unable to tell him what I wanted. I was mindless. Luckily, he knew exactly what I needed.

"Come for me, Lauren. Give me that greedy cunt." At his words I exploded. He kept up his slow, unrelenting pace, my orgasm continuing for what seemed like forever. I was finally starting to come down when he turned the vibrator on higher and pinched my nipple in a tight grasp, not letting go. I was immediately spiraled into another orgasm, clenching and unclenching around him and the plug. "Yes. Give me more," he groaned in my ear. I came down fully this time, but he was still moving inside me. He actually was increasing his pace. He released my breast and instead pulled the plug out almost all the way before shoving it back in, alternating it with his strokes. I felt myself reluctantly building again.

"Please, Phoenix. I don't think I can again."

"Yes you can. You're not even close to done yet," he growled, spanking me hard over and over. "You're such a dirty girl. You love it that I'm fucking you with a plug in your ass, don't you?"

"Yes, I do. Please," I begged, though for what I wasn't sure.

"Come again." At his command I exploded around him, collapsing on the bench, spent. "Sweetness, you're going to come one more time when I do, okay?" I whimpered at his demand, unsure if I could.

He unbound my hands and flipped me over, laying me back on the bench and spreading my legs out wide. He entered me again, pushing the vibrator against me and latching his lips around my nipple. His pace had increased and he started becoming more animalistic with his thrusting and I knew he was close.

"Please, Lauren. Give me one more. I know you can," he pleaded with me, his voice strained.

My hands made their way to my breasts as I tweaked my nipples, trying to push myself over the edge. He reached around and pulled the plug out and I toppled over, screaming his name as I came. He followed immediately after, groaning his release, stilling and pulsing inside of me. He lay on me for a minute, both of us catching our breath. He pulled back and gave me a sweet kiss before moving off of me and helping me sit up.

"What did you think?" he asked, gently undoing the bonds around my chest.

"It was intense," I said, blushing, not able to meet his eyes.

"Did you like it?" he asked.

"Yes" was all I said, suddenly shy.

"Oh, come on, sweetness. After what we just did, you're embarrassed now?"

"It was just different. I've never done anything like that before. It felt wrong and dirty, but I liked it so much. I don't think I've ever come that many times before."

"Did it actually feel wrong and dirty, or do you just feel like it *should* feel wrong and dirty?" he asked, genuinely curious.

"Hmm. I'm not sure. My mind is all jumbled right now."

"Don't worry about it, honey. Just stuff to think about later on."

An hour later, I pulled up to our apartment. I was suddenly extremely anxious. I was worried that Anna wouldn't forgive me, and that things were too damaged between us. I took a few deep breaths in the car, centering myself. When I felt somewhat calmer, I headed in.

I went straight to my room to get the box ready. I pulled out the jewelry I had ordered and set the pieces neatly in the box, sorting them into different sections based on what they were. I had also found a card on Etsy that said "Sorry I'm Such an Asshole."

I took another breath and gently knocked on her door. "Anna? Will you come out? I want to talk."

"Go away, Lauren."

"Anna, please?"

I heard a dramatic huff before she cracked the door open.

"What?"

"I'm really sorry, Anna. I feel really awful about how I've acted this week, and I wanted to make it up to you."

"Well, you can't, Lauren."

"Hold on. I have a present for you," I said, handing over the box and card.

She barely even glanced at it before looking at me, stunned. "You think you can just buy me a gift and we'll be all good?"

"Well, I feel really bad, and I'm trying to make it right between us. I've tried giving you space, I've tried talking and apologizing multiple times, I've tried to still be near you and to work things out through yoga, nothing is working. I don't know what else I can do. I had Phoenix make this box for you, and I filled it with pretty jewelry for your piercings." As soon as I said Nix's name, her entire face shut down.

"Are you fucking kidding me? You're trying to make it right with me and you have *him* make me something? I don't want jack shit from him. Or from you for that matter." She shoved the box back into my hands before slamming her door in my face.

I stood there for a full minute, completely stunned. I was afraid this would happen, but I really thought that she would love all of the thought I put into it. It looked like I wouldn't be able to fix things with her after all. I went into my room and sobbed, mourning the loss of a dear friend.

Chapter 18

Phoenix

I texted Lauren a few hours after she left. I wanted to check if she and Anna had made up. I knew that she was really nervous about how Anna would react, and had been really hating the tension between the two of them.

How did it go?

Terrible was all she said. Shit.

I decided to call her instead, needing to see if she was okay. She answered on the third ring.

"Hey." Her voice sounded rough, like she'd been crying.

"Hey, sweetness. What happened?"

"I don't think she's ever going to forgive me, Phoenix. I don't understand. It's like everything I do to try to make it better just makes her more upset with me. I don't know what to do anymore." She barely finished before it sounded like she was trying to stop herself from crying again.

"I'm sorry, baby" was all I told her, not really knowing how to calm her down or make it better.

"Phoenix, I don't know if I can live here anymore."

"Well, you should move in with me then," I said simply. She was so silent on the other end that I was sure I'd lost her. "Lauren? Are you still there?"

"Yes, I'm here," she replied quietly.

"So, what do you think?" I asked nervously.

"You really want to live with me? You don't think it's too soon?" She sounded unsure.

"No, sweetness, I don't think it's too soon. I knew that first night that you were the perfect girl for me, even if you were too scared to admit it."

"Okay," she whispered.

"Okay?"

"Yeah. Okay, I'll move in with you," she said louder this time, a smile in her voice.

"Well, why don't you come back over now? Pack all your clothes and bathroom stuff. Don't worry about any of the big things, you won't need them. We're going to make it official."

She laughed as she said, "Okay. Let me clean up a bit and I'll be over soon."

"Oh, and Lauren?"

"Yes?"

"We're going to christen every surface in our house tonight," I growled before I hung up, letting her think about that while she got ready to finally come home.

An hour and a half later, she arrived at my house, honking as she pulled up. I opened the door and went to go help her with her things. She had four huge trash bags filled with clothes, and a box for all her knickknacks and bathroom stuff. As soon as we got back into the house with everything, she smiled at me, and I scooped her up and spun her around as I kissed her. I couldn't believe she had actually said yes to moving in with me so soon. Not that I was complaining.

"Want some wine?" I asked, figuring drinking would make this a more fun activity.

"Yes, please."

I went to get the beverages, and brought them to the bedroom to find that Lauren was already starting to unpack. I set them down and started to help her, showing her which dresser she could use and clearing a space for her things in my closet. It felt so domestic, something I had only really experienced once, and it didn't feel anything like this.

"So, do you want to talk about what happened?" I asked.

She proceeded to tell me about their conversation and about Anna's reaction. If Lauren was confused as to why she was upset, then I was absolutely perplexed. It made zero sense to me, and frankly, was completely the opposite of what I had come to expect from Anna. I hadn't had a ton of interactions with her, but she was always very lively and happy from what I could tell. There was always the chance that it was all a front, but I still didn't get it.

"Did you tell her you were moving out?" I asked.

"I left her a note. I didn't think she would come out of her room after everything. Plus, I didn't really want to see her or talk to her. I figured she would get even more upset if she knew I was leaving."

"Well, I'm really sorry that things worked out the way they did, but I am very glad that you're here with me," I told her.

"I am too, Phoenix. This feels so natural. As much as I loved Ryan, it didn't ever quite feel this effortless. I feel like I've known you forever."

"Same here, sweetness" was all I said. I was so tempted to tell her I loved her, but it was too soon. I knew it was too soon. I would just have to show her instead.

When we finished unpacking her things, I refilled her wine, and drew her a bath. I knew she'd had a hard day, and I saw her eyeing my huge clawfoot tub when she first walked into my bathroom. I undressed her and helped her into the tub, telling her to enjoy herself and just relax. Then, I left her alone, figuring she needed some time to herself to sort out her feelings.

I went downstairs, got another beer, and turned on *The Office*. Forty-five minutes later, Lauren waltzed in, wearing a long black silk nightgown. She looked like a queen striding around in her kingdom, and it took my breath away.

"Want to watch the show with me for a little bit or should I take you to bed?"

"Let's watch one episode and then bed."

I held my arm out for her. She quickly snuggled into my side, letting out a satisfied sigh as she settled in. We watched the show, content just being in each other's arms.

When it was finished, I turned everything off, grabbed her hand, and led her to our bed. This time, I was going to be gentle with her. I was going to make love to her instead of fuck her. Not only did she need it after the day she'd had, but also because we were sharing this new and exciting experience together and I wanted to show her how much she meant to me.

I gently laid her on the bed and stood above her, just admiring what a beautiful creature she was. I quickly stripped, noticing how her eyes blazed the more I took off. When I was completely naked, I climbed onto the bed with her. My erection was huge and throbbing, but I ignored it. My hands glided down her silk-clad torso, and she shivered. I took a nipple into my mouth over the fabric, knowing that it would be a different sensation for her. Within seconds, she was squirming underneath me.

"Please, Phoenix. Take me. After this afternoon with you, I don't need any more foreplay."

My fingers slid into her cleft, to find her already wet for me. I groaned into her chest as I hiked her nightgown up her body. When her pelvis was exposed, I slowly slid into her. My weight was on my elbows as I looked into her eyes, sheathing myself to the hilt. Her legs had wrapped around my waist and her hands were clawing at me. One hand fisted in my hair, pulling, as the other dragged fingernails down my back.

This time, there was no kink, nothing extra, just the two of us, intertwined, completely absorbed in one another. Usually, it wasn't my thing, but with Lauren, as long as I was inside her, any and all of it was my thing. This connection that I had with her scared the absolute shit out of me, and I wondered if she felt it too.

I tried to maintain my slow pace, but soon she was digging her heels into my ass and begging me to move faster. I didn't have the self-control to deny her. I started picking up speed and she moved with me, impaling herself on me over and over again.

"Are you close, Lauren?"

"Yes, Phoenix. Almost there."

"Touch yourself, sweetness. Give it to me."

She did as I told her, and a minute later, she was detonating around me. I let go, spilling myself inside her, looking into her eyes as I groaned my release.

She fell asleep in my arms a few minutes later, and I lay awake thinking about how I was the luckiest bastard on the planet.

Chapter 19

Anna

I sat in my room and listened to Lauren rummaging around in her space, no doubt cleaning. She tended to do that when she was upset. Finally when she was finished, there was a knock on my door. I didn't feel like talking anymore so I just ignored her. A minute later, I heard the front door close and I knew she was gone for the night. She was probably going to stay with Nix.

The thought made me even more angry, which was saying something, because I felt like I was about to explode. I also cleaned when I was pissed, which was great for the apartment. Once my room was spotless, I had calmed down and was able to examine my feelings a bit better.

Why was I so angry? I knew I was overreacting, but I couldn't help myself. It was like everything out of her mouth just made me that much more upset. I was originally planning on forgiving her fairly soon, but then she kept going to hang out with him, and I couldn't bring myself to do it. I had been so hurt and worried when she blew me off the week prior. I knew she didn't mean to do it, but that almost made it worse. Like I wasn't even on her radar anymore, she just forgot about me, willy-nilly. I felt like she was so much more important to me than I was to her, just like everyone else in my fucking life. There was a reason that I was alone all the time. No one ever stayed. I guess I wasn't the type of girl that you stuck around for.

I needed liquor if I was going to continue down this path. I opened my door to get some wine from the kitchen, and saw the box and card from Lauren on the floor in front of my room. The sight of it brought tears to my eyes. I was such a bitch. But better a bitch than to show her how hurt and upset I truly was. At first when she gave me the present, I still didn't want to forgive her, so I grasped at the first thing I could think of, but when she told me Nix made it, it felt like a slap in the face, a reminder of why she wasn't hanging out with me anymore.

I picked it up to find a note on top. It wasn't the card that she was originally going to give me, and my stomach plummeted when I read the words.

Anna,

I know now that you are never going to forgive me, but I wanted to tell you anyway how sorry I am. I know that I'm the one who ruined our friendship, and I will regret it forever. You have been the best friend a girl could ask for, and you were there for me during the worst time in my life. I wouldn't be the woman I am today without you helping me through it. I will forever be grateful to you.

I know that you don't want me here anymore, so I've decided to give you your space back. I will really miss living with you, and hope that someday we can at least get along again.

All my love,

Lauren

I couldn't believe it. I had ruined the one good relationship I had in my life. I still had Savannah, but she was so wrapped up with Charlie that I didn't get to see her much anymore. I looked down at the gifts she had left. The card made me reluctantly chuckle; it was so Lauren. Apologizing while still being funny. When I looked at the box, I gasped. It was the most beautiful box I had ever seen. The design was absolutely gorgeous, and just my style. I opened it to find a bunch of jewelry for all my piercings. I ran my fingers over the engraving on the inside, feeling even worse about myself. She was my person, and what did I do? Made her feel like she wasn't welcome in our apartment.

Well, I decided I wouldn't ruin it anymore. I would give her space and leave her alone, but if she ever wanted to come back or needed me for anything, I would be there for her in a heartbeat. I hoped she would come back eventually. I hated to think that I had fucked up the one good thing in my life just because I was insecure and jealous.

By this time, I was full-on sobbing. I grabbed the open bottle of wine on the counter and sank to the floor, drowning my sorrows in booze. I started putting on all of the jewelry she had gotten me.

When I was finished with the bottle, and was good and drunk, I looked at Lauren's note again, and everything suddenly made sense. I knew exactly why I had been so angry and upset. I couldn't believe it had taken me so long to figure it out. I ran to the bathroom and emptied the contents of my stomach, my realization flipping my world upside down.

Chapter 20

Lauren

Over the next few weeks, Phoenix and I settled into a rhythm. We had gotten all my knickknacks and little things set up, but the house still felt very Nix to me. Not that I minded, I loved his style, it just didn't quite feel like my space yet. With Anna, it had been different because we shared the same exact style, so our apartment just felt like a place that I had already decorated. Plus I hadn't brought anything besides my clothes and a few knickknacks. I brought this up to him one morning.

"Hey, handsome. I would like to go shopping for some more stuff to put around the house this week. Would you want to come with me?"

"Sure, sweetness. You don't like my taste?" he teased.

"I do like it, but I want some of my style reflected too," I told him.

"I'm just kidding, Lauren. Of course we can do that. I want this place to feel like home for you," he said, stroking my cheek and making me smile. It had been so nice living here with him. I loved waking up next to someone again, and to settle into a routine. Something as simple as brushing our teeth together in the morning felt so normal and domestic. I had missed that a lot since Ryan passed.

"I would also like to set up a little yoga/meditation studio. Can I take the empty bedroom upstairs?"

"Of course. That's a great idea. It's like that space was just waiting for you to come in and transform it. I have some time this morning if you want to go today. I don't have to go to work until three."

"Okay!" I exclaimed, suddenly excited to get started.

We both got ready and drove to American Furniture Warehouse, deciding to start there since they had furniture and decor. Soon, we were browsing the aisles, looking for anything that fit me.

I came across a huge deep purple chair. It was one of those that you sink into and could stay curled up in for hours at a time with a cozy blanket. I sat down in it and immediately felt the urge to do so. It was by far the comfiest thing I had ever sat on in my life.

"I'm getting this," I told Phoenix, not caring if he liked it or not. "I'm going to put it in my studio." It would be perfect for a reading nook.

I also found a nice bookcase. Phoenix noticed me lingering around it. I liked it, but I wasn't sure if I needed it or not. "I could build you something better than that," he whispered in my ear.

"Really? You'd build me a bookcase?" I asked, slightly shocked. I figured that it would take him too much time. Time that he could be working on stuff that would make him money.

"Of course, sweetness. I built Anna that box for you. Why wouldn't I be willing to make you something?"

"Well, it was just so small. This is much bigger. I thought you wouldn't want to spend time making it when you could make something to sell."

"Lauren, I would love to make you something. I've actually been thinking about what I could make you."

"Well, I would love that. Thank you," I said, slightly teary as I gave him a kiss.

We continued on our little trip through the store, making note of all the things I liked, especially the things we both really liked. By the time we left, we had spent a shit ton of money, but had gotten a lot of really great items.

I bought the purple chair, multiple pieces of artwork for the living room, bedroom, and studio, an end table for all the stones I was going to get, twinkle lights for the studio, and some throw blankets. Overall, it was a very successful trip. There were a few things that I still had to go get, but I could do that on my own. I figured Phoenix wouldn't really be interested in shopping for more bohemian stuff for the yoga room.

He dropped me off at home before heading in to work. We brought most of the stuff home, but the chair would need to be delivered separately. Once we unloaded, Nix headed to work, and I drove to a stone shop down the street. Anna had introduced me to the use of stones and had them all over the apartment, but I didn't have any of my own yet.

I walked in and was completely overwhelmed by what I saw. There was every type of stone you could ever imagine. They had them in every size and shape you could want. Pieces ranged from $3 to $300. I wished I could buy them all, but I had to pace myself. It took years to build collections like Anna's. I tried to remember all the stones she had told me about and what they were good for, but off the top of my head, the only ones I could remember were amethyst (good for anxiety), and rose quartz (good for love, healing, and peace). I bought a huge amethyst cathedral that I was planning on putting either in the living room or bedroom, a smaller amethyst cluster for the studio, along with a midsize rose quartz. As I was checking out, they also recommended I get clear quartz (good for setting intentions and spiritual growth), and obsidian (good for absorbing negative energies and grounding).

I then stopped at a Tibetan shop next door. There, I found a tapestry with all of the chakras on it with all different colors, some incense and a beautiful incense burner—the smoke poured down from leaf to leaf before pooling at the bottom—a singing bowl, a buddha statue, and a lotus-shaped Himalayan salt lamp.

When I was finished, I went home, excited to set up everything that I had gotten that day. I loved Anna's studio, but this one would be completely my own, with pieces I had picked out myself. I worked the rest of the day getting it set up. By the time I was finished, I stood back and admired my work. It was perfect, and I could clearly see where the bookshelf and chair would go. I took a deep breath in, feeling the calm of the space around me, and I started crying. It was a cleansing type of cry, and I let go of all the shit that was bottled up inside me.

Once I was done, I took out my sage and palo santo, and cleansed the space and any negative energy that I had gotten rid of. By the time I had finished, it was late, but I felt newly energized getting everything set up.

I poured myself a glass of wine and looked around the house, wondering where we could put the other items we bought today. There was a piece that I definitely wanted to go in the bedroom, and another that I thought would look perfect in the basement. The one for the bedroom was a bronze metal sun, with a mirror in the middle of it. The picture for the basement we didn't get at AFW, and there was no way they would ever sell it. I found it online the week before and it just happened to arrive here the same day. It was a black-and-white photo of a couple. It was zoomed in so you couldn't see their faces. The woman was topless, and there was water dripping from her. The man had his hands wrapped around her, one around her throat, and the other cradling and caressing her naked breast. It was very classy, but still extremely sensual.

While I was at it, I decided to hang those pieces, not wanting them to sit around forever. The sun, I hung up over our bed, dead center. I stood back and admired it; it really tied the room together. The erotic photo I hung on the wall next to the sex swing. The black-and-white was perfect for the style of the space.

I had also gotten us a few throw blankets, because like a typical man, Nix had zero of them around the house, and that was just unacceptable in my opinion. I loved having something to snuggle up underneath when we were on the couch watching a movie. I got a brown and tan fake fur one for the living room, which went great with the brown leather couches. I got another one for my studio that was big and gray. It was chunky, knitted, and so comfy. I was going to put it on my purple chair as soon as it was delivered. I had always wanted to make one of these, but I had no idea how to go about it, considering I had absolutely no skills in the craft department. For now, I folded it and set it where my chair would be. I also got one more for the bedroom. It was just a plain white fleece to offset the gray comforter that he already had in there.

Since Nix was gone for the night, I decided to camp out on the couch and watch all the girly shit I wanted. I made myself some caramel corn, curled up with my wine, and my new blanket and turned on *P.S. I Love You*. This movie always made me cry, and I had been too stuck in my own traumatic incident with Ryan to watch it until now. Halfway through the movie, I started to compare it with my own life. Of course the situations were completely different, but I saw a lot of myself in Hilary Swank's character. When she slept with the first man after her husband, I broke down in sobs, something I had never done at this part, because now I understood exactly how she felt, ready but guilty and scared.

When the movie ended, I had a whole new outlook that I didn't have before, and I felt the same open-ended hope that she had at the end of the movie. My life was finally moving on, and I had figured out what I wanted. There was only one thing left to do. It was time to finally visit Ryan's grave.

The next day, I woke up next to Phoenix. He was passed the fuck out, which was understandable, considering he had probably only gotten home five hours prior. I must've been exhausted too because I didn't even stir when he came to bed. I looked out the window to find it pouring, which seemed appropriate since I was about to go to the cemetery. I left Nix a note on the pillow, doubting he would even wake up before I got back, but just in case. I dressed in a dark plum dress and black boots, knowing it was going to be muddy. I stopped by the grocery store on the way there and got two bouquets of white lilies.

I pulled up to the cemetery and got out, bringing my umbrella with me. As I walked the short distance to his grave, I realized I hadn't been here since the funeral. Even then, I wouldn't say I was "here." I had been too overcome with grief. I barely even remembered seeing his parents.

When I got to his grave, my breath caught in my throat. Things felt so different, like it was a completely separate lifetime. As happy as I was in my life now, I still missed Ryan with everything I had. I missed being able to talk to him, to laugh with him, to feel comforted by him. I think that was what had hurt the worst when he died, that he was always my comfort, and when I needed that comfort the most, he wasn't here to give it to me. I missed my dear friend.

I no longer felt as if he was my soulmate; I didn't believe in them anymore. I felt as though we had people we were better suited for, and you had to work hard to keep that relationship going. I felt now that he was my light, and that he had led me to this place in my life. This place where I was the best me I could be.

I laid the lilies at the base of his headstone. I had gotten a bouquet for him, and one for our baby. I knew that wherever he was, our baby was with him. I clutched at my stomach, feeling the loss of the little life that was once inside of me. I had been ecstatic when I found out I was pregnant. I always felt like I was meant to be a mother, and as soon as I felt that presence in my womb, I felt complete. I often wondered how it would've been if I hadn't miscarried. Even if Ryan had still died, I would've had a little piece of him in that baby. That was one of the biggest things that I mourned as well. I would never be able to have a baby with Ryan. That opportunity had died right alongside him. I would never know who our children would be, if they would have his looks and my personality, or my eyes and his smile.

Tears silently ran down my cheeks as I reached out to touch the stone. Suddenly, I felt his energy surrounding me. I gasped as I smiled, breathing in his presence.

"Hello, Ryan. I've missed you," I said, eager to talk to him again. "Life is so different for me now. I'm a completely different woman. I finally feel like I've gotten pieces of myself back since you left, but I'm not the same. Sometimes I miss that woman, but most of the time I'm grateful that I was able to grow and find out who I was always supposed to be." As I spoke, I felt a deep contentment settle inside of me, and I knew that this was right.

I continued to talk, not realizing how much time was passing. I told him everything, about Phoenix, about Anna, about my new yoga journey. All of it. I poured everything out at his feet and genuinely felt as though he were here listening, hanging on my every word. I laughed and cried and everything in between. I must have been there for two hours or more, just spilling out every detail of my life I could think of since he died. I was freezing and shivering, my clothes damp from all the moisture in the air, but I didn't care.

When I finally finished, I told him goodbye, said that I missed him and that I would visit again, and kissed the headstone. When I turned around, Phoenix was standing by my car, just watching and waiting for me. I didn't know how long he'd been there, and I didn't care. I was leaving my past behind and looking forward toward my future.

When I got to him, he swiped his thumb under my eye, wiping away any stray tears, as I looked up at him and smiled.

"You okay, sweetness?" he asked, concerned.

"Yeah, baby. I'm okay. I've been needing to do that for a long time."

"You ready to go home?" he asked, wrapping his arms around me.

"With you? Always," I replied.

Chapter 21

Phoenix

One month later...

"Sweetness, you ready?" I yelled at her, loading up the car with our things.

"Yes! I'm coming. Sorry," she said, exasperated and breathless as she ran toward me.

"Took you long enough," I teased.

"I know. I'm sorry! I had to get all my shit and triple-check that everything in the house was turned off."

"Well, get that sweet ass in the car so we can get movin'," I said, slapping her backside as she walked past me, making her squeal in surprise.

We both hopped in the car, made a quick stop at the gas station to fuel up and to get some last-minute road trip snacks, then we were off. I started out driving, with Lauren in the passenger seat, who was the perfect copilot.

"What do you want to start off listening to?" she asked, her fingers poised over her phone, ready to get the music going.

"How about Weezer?" I asked.

"Yes. Which album?"

"*Pinkerton*," I said. That was my brother's favorite road trip album, so whenever I went on one I had to play it, otherwise it didn't feel right.

After we'd been driving for about a half hour, Lauren turned to me and asked, "So, are you nervous to meet my family?"

"Of course. What sane man wouldn't be?"

"Oh, stop. They're going to love you. They aren't the intimidating type."

"Oh, I doubt that. All men are protective over their little girls. Especially one that has had her heart broken fairly recently."

"Fair point, but don't worry. They will love you," she repeated.

We alternated driving throughout the day, switching about halfway through. We decided we would break the drive to Michigan into two separate days, stopping for the night in Iowa. We found a little motel off the highway when we didn't feel like driving anymore. It was nice enough, small but cozy. Plus there weren't very many people there so that was nice. We had gotten dinner before the motel so as soon as we got into the room, we crashed.

We slept soundly all through the night, and decided not to set an alarm, just waking up whenever we felt like it. In the morning, we woke at nine, just in time to get the continental breakfast from the hotel. When we were all full, packed, and showered, we headed back out.

We spent the day laughing, singing, playing games, and taking turns sleeping. It was the perfect day. I had always loved road trips, but this one was particularly special.

We finally pulled up to Lauren's childhood home at around six. Just in time for dinner, like we'd planned. We got out of the car and stretched, and her family immediately came running out to greet us. Lauren squealed, a sound I had never heard from her mouth, before running up to her mom and giving her a huge hug. Then she did the same with her dad and sister. With the whole family standing next to each other, I could definitely see the resemblance. She and her sister looked like carbon copies of their mom, with the exception of the eyes and jawline that they seemed to have gotten from their dad. They also had the same exact nose, but it didn't seem to come from either of their parents.

I walked forward, holding my hand out and saying, "Hello, everyone. I'm Nix."

Her mom walked up to me, ignored my outstretched hand, and wrapped me in a warm hug. "Nix. Lauren has told us so much about you. I'm so glad that you could come all the way here. We've all been so excited to meet you."

Her sister was next, giving me the same treatment. Then her dad came up. I was originally fairly nervous to meet him, but he had a welcoming expression on his face and he grasped my hand firmly before patting me on the back.

"Good to meet you, sir," I said to him.

"No need for sir. Just call me Jack. And feel free to call Lauren's mother Shannon. We're very informal here."

"Well, Jack, Shannon, thank you so much for having me. And I've heard so much about you, Kate. I'm so glad to be here," I said emphatically. Kate blushed under my attention, probably since I was so much older than her. Lauren told me that her sister was six years younger than she was. When she was little she had wanted to be just like her big sister, apparently, copying everything that Lauren did.

"So, should we all go inside and start dinner? Everything is almost ready," Shannon said.

"Mom, Phoenix and I are going to put our stuff away and then get cleaned up from the drive. We will be down for dinner in twenty minutes," Lauren said, for which I was grateful. I wanted to get a little settled and have a chance to take a quick shower, washing off the day.

"Sure, darling. We'll wait for you. Take your time."

We grabbed our bags and lugged them up to Lauren's childhood bedroom. As soon as I stepped in, I could see her teenage self spending all her time in here. There were music posters all over the walls, a bulletin board full of pictures of her and her friends, a small TV with a DVD player and VCR built into it, and twinkle lights surrounding a bed with a dark blue comforter with a huge sun on it. Luckily, she also had her own attached bathroom so we didn't have to share with anyone.

"Wanna take a quick shower?" she asked.

"Yes. I feel disgusting."

"Same here," she agreed before leaning over to turn the water on and put up her hair. We both stripped off our clothes and got under the spray. She moaned as the hot water cascaded over her, and I watched the water's path down her body, mesmerized. Without thinking, I pulled her against me and licked the liquid off her neck.

"Oh, God. You can't do that now. We don't have time before dinner," she reprimanded, but made no move to pull away from me.

"Oh, come on. We can be quick," I reasoned, thrusting my growing erection against her stomach.

"Fine. But if you get my hair wet, I'll be pissed," she warned.

"I won't. Turn away from me," I said. As soon as she did, I thrust into her wet heat, groaning. This would never get old.

We still made it downstairs for dinner twenty minutes later. Her mother had the table set, including a glass of red wine for Lauren, and a Heineken for me. At my surprised look, Shannon said, "Lauren told me," with a wink and smile. I thanked her before sitting down next to Lauren. Her mom had made lasagna with Caesar salad and garlic bread. Apparently, this meal was a staple in their house. Shannon had gotten the recipe from her mom just as Lauren had gotten it from Shannon. When the time came, I was sure our daughter would learn it from Lauren too.

Oh. Shit.

Where had that thought come from? Way too soon for those kinds of ideas. And not a great time to be having them either, meeting her family for the first time. I took a big swig of my beer and shook my head to clear away that train of thought.

"You okay, Nix?" Jack asked.

"Yes. Just a little tired from the drive is all."

"So, what do you guys have planned while you're here?" Kate asked.

"Well, mostly just hang around here with you guys. I would like to see Jessa while I'm here, and was maybe thinking the three of us could have a girls' day? What do you think, Kate? You like Jessa, right?" Jessa was Lauren's best friend from high school. They stayed close over the years and she came out to visit after Ryan passed.

"Oh, yes, please. I would love to. I've been so busy with school stuff that a girls' day would be so much fun!" she exclaimed, clearly excited at being invited to hang out with the older girls.

"Nix, do you fish? Would you like to go out on the lake with me that day?" her father asked me.

"That sounds like a great time, Jack. I love fishing," I answered. It would be a great opportunity to get to know him better.

"Perfect! I'll text Jessa and see what day works for her," Lauren said excitedly.

"So, Kate, what are you in school for?" I asked.

"Psychology. I only have one year left," she said, seeming a little nervous at speaking to me directly.

"Oh, that's awesome! What got you interested in that?"

"I find people interesting. I like being able to analyze their behavior."

It was funny to me that while Lauren and her sister looked so similar, they were very different. Lauren was very outgoing and personable. She had also chosen fields that weren't typical, they were a little more creative and based on feeling or intuition, very right brain. Kate was a little awkward and shy, and had chosen a career path that was more "acceptable" in society, something a little more logical, more left brain. Who knows? Maybe that's why they got along so well, because they were so opposite.

"So, Lauren tells us that you're a fireman?" Shannon asked.

"Yes, ma'am. My dad was one so that was the field I chose. He always encouraged it."

"But, he's also been selling some pieces on Etsy. He's a woodworker and makes some really beautiful things," Lauren added, smiling at me.

"Oh really? Like what?" Jack asked.

"Honestly, whatever I feel like making. Some big pieces and some small ones. Boxes, bowls, end tables, bookcases. You name it."

"Wow. Well, for Christmas you can always make us something," Shannon said.

"Mom! That's a bit presumptuous," Lauren scolded.

"Well, I'm just saying. I would love to have something he made for us in the house." Lauren rolled her eyes at her, chuckling.

"Duly noted, Shannon. Any requests?" I asked.

"Surprise me, Nix."

We spent the rest of the evening chatting and getting to know one another. I felt very comfortable in their home and with them. They felt a lot like my family, and I had a feeling that our families would get along really well.

By the end of the night, Jessa had texted back that she would like to spend time with the girls the next day, so they made plans. Jack and I made our own plans to go fishing. We originally talked about going to one of the smaller ponds, but since I had never been to Lake Michigan, he told me we had to go there, that it was something you had to see when you came to this state.

With all our plans made, we went to bed, exhausted after our trip. We fell asleep as soon as our heads hit the pillows.

Chapter 22

Lauren

The next day, Kate and I met Jessa at our favorite brunch place. Kate was finally able to drink, which was nice since we all decided to get mimosas. What was brunch without mimosas? After we settled in and ordered our food, we all started catching up.

"So, how are you? You seem much better than when I last saw you," Jessa noticed.

"I'm doing so great. I am definitely a hundred times better than when you came out after the accident. Things feel like they're just falling into place."

"How's yoga going?" Kate asked.

"It's perfect. It feels like it has been my calling all along."

"Are you still living with that Anna girl?" Jessa asked.

"Well, that's actually the only thing that's not great." I proceeded to tell them everything about the huge fight that had broken out. I answered their questions as best I could considering that I myself didn't really understand what had happened. "So, now I'm living with Nix. Things are great and I'm glad I'm there, but I just really hate the way it came to be."

"It kinda sounds like she's jealous," Jessa said.

"Jealous of what though?" I asked, confused.

"Well, you finally feel happy with everything. You found your calling and you love work, you found a great man even after everything that you've been through. Maybe she's not as happy as she's always appeared, and she's jealous that you're not sad and depressed because of the accident anymore. Plus, she's never been in a relationship the whole time you've known her, from what you've told us. She's also probably jealous that you found someone else even after losing Ryan."

I thought about that for a minute. I had always felt like Anna wasn't as happy-go-lucky as she wanted everyone to think. Not to mention that she never talked about her past. I didn't even know where she'd grown up or anything about her family. Whenever Savannah or I asked, she would always make a dismissive comment and then change the subject. It was definitely possible that she was upset that I had found happiness when she hadn't.

"Yeah, you're probably right. So, what should I do?" I asked.

"I don't think there's anything you can do. You've already done everything you can. Now it's up to her. She'll have to decide if your friendship is more important to her than all of that."

"Ugh. Okay. I just hate waiting and not being able to do anything."

"I know, but I think she'll come around. And if she doesn't, then she was never a real friend in the first place."

"Okay, well, enough about me. How are things going with you?"

"They're good. Still working for the same company. It's not my passion or anything, but it pays the bills. And Bobby and I just celebrated our one year anniversary," Jessa said. I felt a twinge of guilt. She had invited me to the wedding, but I wasn't in a good place mentally to go, not to mention that it was so far away. I had told her that I wasn't able to get the time off work. She understood, but now I wished I had gone.

"That's amazing! Jess, I'm so sorry I wasn't able to make it to the wedding. I didn't feel ready to see you guys get married, especially since you've been together since high school like Ryan and me. It would've been like watching us get married but not being a part of it. I couldn't do it," I told her, tearing up.

"Lauren, stop. It's okay. I knew you weren't going to come to the wedding. I knew it was too soon for you. I'm not upset. I promise," she reassured me, squeezing my hand.

After that, we kept it lighthearted, talking about Kate's school and her new boyfriend. We ate and drank and laughed. When we were done, we decided to get pedicures and then see a movie. We saw a girly one, figuring our significant others would never want to see it. It was only three o'clock when the movie finished, so we walked around the mall for a while, mostly just window shopping, until we came across Victoria's Secret.

"Ooh, let's go in! I could use some new lingerie," Jessa said.

"I think I'll meet you guys later," Kate mumbled quietly.

"Hell no, Kate. You're coming in here with us," I said, dragging her behind me.

"No, Lauren. It makes me uncomfortable. I've never been in one of these stores before."

"So, do you not have any lingerie?" Jessa asked her.

Kate didn't answer, looking at the floor and blushing instead.

"Have you slept with your new boyfriend yet?" I asked. This probably wasn't the best way to go about this, but I'd had some drinks and we were having fun.

"Lauren!"

"Well, have you?"

"Yes, okay? I have. I just am not very good at this stuff."

"Well, that's why you have us. You should get something sexy to wear for him. It's super fun. I promise," I said, trying to convince her.

"Okay, fine."

I squealed as I pulled her into the store with me. We looked through the whole store, making her try on everything. By the time we left, we each had a sexy item for our men. Kate had gotten a white baby doll, which I'm sure had the innocent vibe she was going for. Jessa had gotten a deep red lace one-piece. It was elegant and incredibly sexy at the same time. I ended up with a mint green lace corset. Not the super tight ones no one can breathe in though. It also had the attachments for stockings at the bottom, which I also bought.

By the time we left, we had spent way too much money, but we were all happy and laughing, including Kate, who ended up loving the store and the piece she bought. She was really excited to be able to wear it for Chris when they got together later that week.

It was the first time she and I had ever done something like this together, and I really loved it. I had always gotten along with her, but she was quite a bit younger than me, so we had never really bonded quite like this before. I guess she was old enough now that she felt like a good friend as opposed to just an annoying younger sister.

We left and I gave Jessa a big hug, telling her that it was so good to see her and that I missed her. She told me that she and Bobby were thinking about planning a trip to come see me in Colorado and that she would get back to me when they talked about dates. Kate and I climbed into her car and she drove us back home.

"Kate, I really love you. You're a great sister, and I'm so glad that you're my family."

"Thanks, Lauren. I feel the same way about you," she said a little awkwardly. This was different for us.

We spent the rest of the drive blasting cheesy music and singing loudly and laughing our asses off. We had the windows rolled down and I closed my eyes at the feel of the humid Michigan air swirling around me and flipping my hair around. I hadn't realized how much

I missed being home. I hadn't been here since before the accident, nervous about coming back without having Ryan with me.

Now that I was here, it didn't feel depressing like I thought it would. It felt like home. Like a breath of fresh air. Not that I would ever want to move back here, but I missed it.

Kate pulled up to the house half an hour later, and we went inside to find the boys had returned from their fishing trip, and Mom was prepping their catch for dinner. I went up to my bedroom to find Phoenix in the shower.

"Hey, baby," I said as I walked into the bathroom.

"Hey, sweetness. How was your girls' day?"

"Fantastic. It was really nice to have some time with both of them. Oh, and I got some new lingerie for you," I told him.

"Well, you'll have to wait 'til we're home to show me because I'll need to give it proper attention, and I won't be able to do that here," he growled.

"I guess I can wait. How was fishing with my dad?" I asked. I had been slightly anxious about it all day. I figured they would get along great, but it made me a little nervous that I couldn't be there to see their interaction.

"It was awesome. He took me to a great spot. The view was incredible and we both caught some fish. Your mom is preparing them for dinner now."

"Yeah, I saw. They look delicious. You're like my own personal caveman, catching my dinner for me," I teased.

"You. Naked. With me. Now," he said in a caveman voice, making me laugh. I quickly stripped and got in the shower with him. We washed each other and made out just a little before getting out. As we were getting dressed, Mom knocked on the door.

"Dinner's ready, kids!" she shouted on the other side of the wood.

We quickly got dressed and headed downstairs. Dinner was delicious and fresh. Mom always knew the secret to fish, soaking it in milk for a while before cooking it, taking the fishy taste out. She then cooked it in butter, white wine, garlic, and lemon.

We all hummed in approval as we ate. I thanked Mom for cooking and the boys for catching. After dinner, we all sat around the living room, reminiscing, talking, and laughing. Of course Dad told the story of the time that we went into the music store and I started organizing the CDs. I was six. Phoenix laughed and chimed in with his own childhood stories.

We spent the next few days enjoying the company, and as I looked at Phoenix with my family, everything felt right.

Chapter 23

Phoenix

We pulled up to the house a week later, exhausted but content. Overall, it was a great trip and I was happy to have met Lauren's family. They seemed equally pleased to meet me, and we had a wonderful time getting to know each other.

We brought our things inside and started getting ready for bed, tired from the drive. As we were brushing our teeth next to each other, Lauren looked at me and smiled, a loving look on her face. She looked tempted to say something, but before she did, she shook her head slightly and spit out her toothpaste.

"What were you going to say?" I asked after I spit out my own.

"I'm just glad you came with me. It was nice having everyone I care about together," she said. I thought for a minute she was going to tell me she loved me, but I guess she wasn't quite ready yet.

"I'm glad too, sweetness."

As soon as we fell into bed, we passed out. We were so tired from all the driving and the activities that we had done while in Michigan. Unfortunately, after taking so much time off, we both had to work as soon as we returned, and when we got up the next morning, we were just as tired as when we went to sleep. Lauren had to work earlier than I did, at eight thirty. I didn't have to go in until ten, but I still woke up when she did. While she was getting ready, I made us both some coffee and brought it to her in the bathroom. She wasn't a huge fan of eating breakfast, usually opting to just bring a banana with her to work, so I just made myself some eggs and toast.

A half an hour later, she came out looking beautiful, but worn out.

"Fuck. Why didn't I take another few days off? Oh, right? Because I need money," she said, talking herself into going to work.

"It'll be fine, sweetness. We'll both go do some short shifts and then we'll come home and I'll make dinner and we can watch anything you want," I told her.

"Anything I want? That's a dangerous promise, sir."

I growled, slapping her ass before giving her a quick kiss. "Go," I said.

She smiled, filling up her to-go mug with more coffee before heading out the door.

I took a quick shower after breakfast and changed into jeans and a T-shirt. I went into work once I was ready. For the most part, it was a slow day, meaning the guys and I basically hung around the station, bullshitting. Charlie was there, which was nice, considering we hadn't seen much of each other lately.

"Hey, man. How'd your trip go?" he asked.

"It was awesome. Her family is great. Nothing like Savannah's family," I said, remembering the first time Charlie met her parents, and grateful that it wasn't me. "Speaking of which, have you guys seen or talked to them since?"

"Nope. For like a week after, I think Savannah got some calls from her mom, but she didn't take any of them, and then she ended up blocking her because she didn't want to have anything to do with them."

"I don't blame her. They sound like a shitshow."

141

"They are," he said. "Oh, hey. I've been meaning to ask you, does Lauren know that we were the ones at the scene and that you were in the ambulance with her?"

The blood drained from my face. "No. She doesn't know. Why?"

"Well, Savannah mentioned the accident the other day, and I was just curious if she knew. I wondered if that was one of the reasons you guys ended up hooking up in the first place, 'cause there was some connection. That's all."

I took a deep breath to calm myself down. I had never told Lauren that because I didn't want to bring up the accident to her. Plus I didn't think she would've been too happy about me seeing her that way. And then of course there was the whole thing with her thinking I had been Ryan, but there was no way she would ever remember that. She had been delirious.

"No, she doesn't know. Can you keep it to yourself? I don't want it to upset her," I asked.

"Sure, man. You might want to tell her on your own though."

"Thanks for the advice" was all I said. There was no way I was going to tell her. I wasn't about to fuck up the best thing that had ever happened to me.

I got home that night at five. Lauren was already there, sitting on the couch and drinking a glass of wine.

"Hey, sweetness. How was your day?"

"It was so long, but I'm home now with you so I'm happy," she said, smiling up at me.

I gave her a lingering kiss before making my way to the kitchen to start dinner. I opened the fridge to find nothing there. I had totally forgotten that we had gotten rid of everything before we left for Michigan so that it wouldn't spoil while we were gone.

"There's no food in the house. Pizza?"

"Oh my God. Yes. That sounds delicious!"

I put in an order on my phone, getting us a supreme pizza with stuffed crust (Lauren's favorite), wings, and cinnamon bread. I then opened up a beer and took a seat next to her on the couch.

"So, what did you decide on to watch tonight?" I asked.

"I think I want to watch *Outlander*. I haven't watched it since Ryan passed, since that was the show that we'd watch together, but I think I'm ready now."

"Okay, sweetness. Whatever you want. I haven't seen it."

"I haven't seen much of it. Ryan and I only got a few episodes in before the accident, but I loved it."

We got everything cued up and started watching. Halfway through the first episode, the pizza came, and we loaded our plates up before continuing. We both loved the show, and soon became addicted. We binged three episodes straight before turning in for the night. By the end of the third one, Lauren was where she and Ryan had left off, but had forgotten what had happened since it had been so long.

We went to bed that night content and full.

I woke up in the middle of the night to Lauren bolting up in bed, breathing hard before breaking down into sobs.

"Lauren, baby, what's wrong?" I asked.

She shook her head at me before throwing the covers off, dashing to the bathroom, and emptying the contents of her stomach in the toilet. I hovered over her, holding her hair out of the way and stroking her back soothingly. When she was finished, she flushed the toilet, and rinsed her mouth before blowing her nose and wiping her eyes.

"Sweetness, tell me what's wrong," I said, her silence making me anxious.

"I had a dream. A memory really" was all she said, avoiding eye contact.

My stomach plummeted. Had she remembered what happened in the ambulance?

"What was it? Talking about it will help," I said as I guided her back to bed and nudged her chin with my fingers so she would look at me.

"It was right before the accident," she said, making me nearly sigh in relief. "I remember what happened and why we were driving. Ryan and I were watching *Outlander* on our day off together. It was the episode you and I just watched. When it was over, I went to the bathroom, only to find a rush of blood coming out of me. I started crying and screaming for Ryan. He picked me up, and put me in the car before rushing to get to the hospital. On the drive, I started feeling really faint and dizzy. The last thing I remember before passing out was Ryan looking at me with a very worried expression and telling me to hold on." By the end of her recount, she was sobbing uncontrollably, breaking down right before my eyes.

I knew saying anything wouldn't soothe her, so instead I took her in my arms, and rocked her back and forth, running my hand through her hair. Eventually she quieted, and I went to get her a box of tissues and a glass of water. She gratefully took both from me, cleaning up her face a bit. When she was finished, we both lay back down and I pulled her as tight as I could against me. I wasn't great with words, but I could give her this. We went to sleep like that, cradled against one another.

Chapter 24

Lauren

The next few days were rough as I processed what happened. I couldn't decide if it was better or worse that I had had a miscarriage before the accident. I felt very conflicted about it. On one hand, I felt relieved because I knew that our baby wasn't meant to be brought into this world no matter what, so the miscarriage wasn't because of the accident, but on the other hand, if I hadn't miscarried, we wouldn't have been in the car rushing to the hospital and never would have gotten in the accident to begin with.

Phoenix was very patient with me, comforting me when I needed it, and just generally being there for me. There were a couple of times that he seemed anxious or had a worried look on his face. I was sure it was because he was concerned about me, but another part of me whispered that wasn't the only reason.

A few nights later, we finally decided to watch the show again. I still loved it and wanted to see what happened. Besides, I had already watched the episode that triggered my nightmare, so now that we were past it, I figured I would be fine.

We went to sleep that night like we did every night, his front to my back, spooning. As I drifted off, I had a feeling that things would be different in the morning.

My dream started out the same as the last one, and as soon as it began, my stomach sank because I didn't want to relive this memory. No matter what I did, I couldn't wake myself up.

I thought it would end the same way it did last time, me staring at Ryan's face and feeling us get hit right before I lost consciousness, but after a minute of nothingness, another memory came flooding in.

I was riding in an ambulance, an extreme pain in my midsection. My first thought was that I must be in labor. Excited, I opened my eyes to find Ryan hovering over me.

"Ryan, are we going to have our baby? Is that why we're in an ambulance?" I asked.

"Yes, baby. Now just relax and get some rest before we get there," he said soothingly.

"Okay, honey. I can't wait to meet our little one," I said, elated.

I pulled his face down to kiss me before I went back to sleep, but as I pulled away, it wasn't Ryan's loving face looking down at me, it was Phoenix's.

I woke in a sweat and I looked over at the man I was falling in love with. I originally thought this dream was another memory, but it was impossible. Ryan was killed on impact. My mind had to be playing tricks on me. Maybe I was still feeling some sort of guilt toward Ryan for being with Phoenix? I wasn't sure, but I didn't want to dwell on this dream. It didn't mean anything. I went back to sleep, curled around him.

A week had passed since my dream. I had told myself that I wasn't going to dwell on it, but no matter what I did, it kept coming back to me, over and over. I could tell that Phoenix had noticed because he kept giving me strange looks. I kept thinking that he was going to ask me what was wrong, but he never did. We just went about our lives like nothing was wrong.

I felt like a robot. I would go into work, cut hair all day, come home, and Phoenix and I would watch TV on the couch without saying much to each other. He seemed just as nervous and in his head as I was, which I thought was strange. Maybe he was worried that I was going to leave him after my flashback of my miscarriage. Whatever it was, things were tense between us, and I didn't like it.

The only time that I got some relief was when I went in to teach my yoga class. Here, everything felt calm and just as it should be. The scent of lavender teased my nostrils, and I inhaled it deeply. I also burned some palo santo when I got there to cleanse everything, me included.

When I came home after my class, Phoenix was sitting in the living room.

"Sweetness, will you tell me what's been bothering you? It's starting to worry me."

I sat down next to him and took a deep breath before diving in. "I had another dream. I told myself it wasn't a big deal and that there's no way it could be real, but I can't let it go." At my words, I saw him visibly pale. "I had a dream that I was in the ambulance getting taken to the hospital when I woke up to see Ryan over me, telling me that we were on our way to have our baby. After I pulled him down for a kiss, his face transformed into yours. I don't know what it means. Like maybe I'm still feeling some guilt for being in another relationship when he's gone? I don't know," I finished quietly.

"Lauren, it wasn't just a dream."

"What do you mean?" I asked, completely stunned.

He swallowed hard, avoiding my gaze. "I was there the day of the accident when they pulled you from the car. I hopped in the ambulance with you so that if you woke up you wouldn't be alone, scared and hurt. When you came to, you were clearly hallucinating, you called me Ryan and asked if we were having our baby. I knew you wouldn't remember any of it, so I lied to you. I didn't want to upset you more. I'm so sorry, Lauren. I just wanted to protect you," he said, each word out of his mouth breaking my heart.

"How could you, Phoenix? What gives you the right?" I shouted at him.

"Sweetness, I didn't know what to do. I didn't want to hurt you more by telling you what happened. Especially when I didn't know for sure," he reasoned with me, but I didn't care. I felt so betrayed. Like our whole relationship was a lie.

"Don't you dare call me that," I screeched at him, becoming more manic by the second. "You betrayed me. You kissed me when I thought you were my dead fiancé. You let me believe that we were going to have our baby and live happily ever after when you knew my life was about to come crashing down all around me. And the worst part is that you pursued a relationship with me afterward and never told me about it! What the fuck, Phoenix? I don't even know you," I sobbed.

He came up to me and tried wrapping me in his arms, but I batted him away, not able to stand his touch. "Lauren, please. I'm so sorry," he begged, but as I looked into his eyes, I saw a man I didn't know.

"Phoenix, I can't. I'm sorry. I can't be near you right now," I told him as I went upstairs. Originally, I thought I would just take a shower and stay away from him for the night, but after I got out of the bathroom, I realized I couldn't be in the same house as him. I got dressed, packed a bag, and went downstairs. When he saw me, he bolted up off the couch.

"Lauren, what's going on?" he asked.

"I can't be here, Phoenix. I need to leave. I need time to think."

"No. Lauren, please, no," he pleaded with me.

"I'm sorry, Phoenix. I can't be here. Every time I look at you, I keep seeing Ryan's face morphing into yours. I keep feeling the betrayal of that kiss on my lips. I can't do it right now," I said, my voice breaking at the end.

He nodded sadly, stepping to the side to let me by. I made my way out the door and as I was closing it behind me, I heard him whisper, "Goodbye, Lauren."

I pulled up to Anna's apartment twenty minutes later. I knocked on her door carrying my bag, tears streaming down my face. It opened a minute later with a confused-looking Anna on the other side.

"Lauren?"

"Anna. Can I come in?" I asked, breaking down into sobs.

"Of course, babe," she said, pulling me into her arms and leading me into the apartment.

She took my bag and put it in my room before sitting me on the couch with a big glass of wine.

"What happened?" she asked when we were both settled.

I proceeded to tell her everything, my dreams and Phoenix's reaction, and ultimately the big fight that ended with me leaving. She interjected sometimes, exclaimed at all the right parts, and held my hand through the whole thing.

"Lauren, I'm so sorry," she said, pulling me into her arms. For the longest time I just sat there and cried. When I started to quiet, she pulled away and said, "He's a dickhead anyway. Who needs him?"

I laughed reluctantly. While I was very upset about what happened with Phoenix, it was so nice to have my best friend back. I missed her so much. We spent the night like we used to, drinking wine on the couch watching our favorite shows.

The rest of the week, we caught up and rekindled our friendship. We spent hours talking and drinking. I didn't eat much since I didn't have an appetite, but I did eat some brownies that Anna shoved in my face as we were watching *The Notebook* and bawling in her bed. She also had an enormous bowl of popcorn for the occasion. We spent most nights cuddled in bed together since I hated sleeping by myself. The one night I did sleep alone, I cried myself to sleep and woke up in a panic from not having someone next to me. It almost felt like losing Ryan all over again, except I felt more betrayed. Luckily, I had Anna with me pretty much the whole time, so I wasn't nearly as lonely.

I hadn't continued watching *Outlander*. I felt like every time I watched it, something bad happened. We just stuck to movies that made us cry hysterically to get out all of our emotions and to help us bond.

I found out that Anna had kept the box and all the jewelry I had gotten her. After a day of me being back home, she apologized and said she realized what a bitch she had been, and how she totally understood why I left. Seeing the box again, however, did remind me of Nix, and I couldn't help the heartbreak that followed.

For his part, he didn't bother me relentlessly with calls and texts. He had sent me only one since I left. It came two days later and all it said was "I miss you." I hadn't responded, still not sure if I was ever going to be able to forgive him.

The week continued on, and I felt closer to Anna than ever. It was like our huge fight had strengthened our connection. We did yoga every day together. Some days I led us, other days we just did our own flows, together but separate. We were moving and growing with each other.

As much as I loved Nix's place, there was something very comforting about being back in this apartment. Maybe it was just the camaraderie I felt with Anna, or maybe it was the fact that this was the first place I had lived without Ryan, but either way, I felt serene here.

Maybe Anna and I would just continue to live here with each other for the rest of our lives, I thought...

Chapter 25

Phoenix

It had been a week since Lauren left. I was miserable. Of course I didn't tell anyone what had happened. I wasn't that type of guy. I liked to keep my shit to myself, but I'm sure people could tell. Whenever I was at work I was constantly snapping at people and just generally avoiding everyone, even worse than normal. A few brave souls dared to ask me if something was wrong but got sent cowering in the opposite direction when I glared at them in answer. I overheard some guys talking in the break room one day between calls.

"Dude, I think he got dumped. I've never seen him this pissed before," one guy said.

"Yeah, I've known him for five years and while he's never been the friendliest guy, he's never been like this," another said.

"She must've been something special to get him this worked up." *Yeah, no shit*, I thought.

I walked into the breakroom, stopping the gossip. All three men looked at me, silent, with slightly worried looks on their faces. I didn't blame them for their conversation. I had been pissy and surly lately, even more than normal. It was no wonder they were talking and spouting theories as to why.

I didn't say anything to them, however when I came in, I liked making them sweat. Let them feel just an ounce of my discomfort. I went straight for the coffee machine, poured a large cup, and walked back out.

A call came in and we all got in the truck. The others were joking around and having fun as we were on our way. I couldn't help but glare at them the whole time. I was envious that they were so happy and carefree while I was so bitter. I sat there stewing. All I could think about was the last twenty minutes that happened between Lauren and me, the fight that had broken out, and the sight of her walking out the door with her bags packed. It just kept replaying in my head over and over, driving me crazy. The only other thought I had was wondering why she hadn't responded to me. I had texted her days ago and she hadn't said anything. I felt like a teenage girl. I kept opening our text thread to see if she was going to reply or not. I could see that she had read the message, she just hadn't said anything back.

When I caught myself doing any of these things or thinking so dramatically about her, I rolled my eyes at myself. This wasn't me. I wasn't this weak and stupid. Not since Tiffany. But Tiffany was a whole other story. And a whole other time in my life. I shook my head to get rid of that train of thought. I didn't like thinking about that period. It was a mess and always made me feel inadequate. Although, I would admit that it made me the man I was, for which I was grateful.

I got home from work that night in need of a strong drink. I poured myself some whiskey, something I didn't usually drink, and took a walk around my home. It didn't feel the same without Lauren here. She hadn't been here long, but she'd sure made an impression on both me and the house.

I hadn't moved a single thing. Her yoga studio was the same, I left up all the pictures we bought, I slept on the same side of the bed, and

I had even left her favorite wineglass next to an unopened bottle of wine on the counter. I had convinced myself that she would be back eventually, even if she hadn't returned my text. She just needed time.

I also kept having regrets. I should've told her what had happened. I should've told her I loved her when I had the chance. And then the crazier thoughts. I should've proposed to her. I should've put a baby in her. That way she wouldn't have been able to leave. I knew that my thoughts were overwhelming and irrational, not to mention illogical, but I couldn't help it. I was a mess and I knew it.

A week after that, she finally texted me.

I'm sorry I haven't been in contact. I've had lots of thinking to do, and I still do. I care about you so much, but my faith in you has been compromised. I don't know if I can trust you again...

I understand, and I'm so sorry. I hope you can forgive me. I will wait however long you need me to.

I hated that her text sounded so formal, not at all indicative of our relationship. She felt so distant. I got it, of course, but it still hurt.

I decided to spend most of my time at the gym. It was easier. Here, I had no memories of her, and I was able to get my frustrations and anxieties out in a healthy way. It was actually becoming a bit of an addiction, being here.

One day, I walked in and went straight for the treadmill. Forty-five minutes later, I got off, intending to head for the weights next when someone came up to the machine right next to mine. My eyes widened as surprise struck me. Out of all of the fucking times, this is when I had to run into her. I tried to sneak away before she saw me, but I wasn't that lucky.

"Nix? Is that you?" Tiffany asked.

"Oh, hey, Tiffany," I replied.

I watched her gaze as she raked her eyes over my sweat-clad body appreciatively. When they returned to my face, she looked flustered.

I also took her in, and found that my memory had not been accurate. I had always thought that she was such a beauty, but looking at her, I realized how fake she was. Her hair was bleach blond, so much so that it looked completely fried. She had very brown skin because she went to the tanning salon multiple times a week, while it used to look attractive on her, it was now taking its toll and was looking very leathery. All she wore were extremely short shorts and a sports bra, which wasn't doing much considering her fake tits were about to spill out. She also had a new butterfly tattoo on the front of her hip that looked like it was done by a twelve-year-old girl. My eyes made their way back up to her face to find so much makeup caked on that I could see a line under her chin where it stopped. There was a flirty look crossing her features as she batted her eyelashes at me and twirled a piece of her hay-looking hair around her finger. She must've thought that I was checking her out.

"How have you been?" she asked.

"Fine. How's Daniel?"

"Oh, come on, now. Don't bring that up. It's not even worth mentioning," she cooed.

"Oh really? Not worth mentioning? The fact that you left me a month before our wedding for your ex isn't worth mentioning?" I seethed.

"Nix, I'm so sorry. I've regretted it for six years. I never should have left you. Daniel was a terrible man, and I knew better. I caught him cheating on me six months later, but by then I knew you wouldn't take me back so I didn't call you," she pleaded with me, sounding more and more pathetic by the minute.

"Well, what can I say? Karma's a bitch."

"Please, Nix baby. Let's get out of here and go for a drink or something. Maybe I'll even let you take me home and tie me up," she whispered in my ear as she stroked my biceps.

"No thanks."

"Oh, come on. I know you've missed me. You don't have to play hard to get with me, honey. You've already had me," she coaxed as her hand started drifting down my stomach toward my waistband. I stopped her hand in its tracks and gently pushed her away from me.

"Tiffany, I can honestly say that I want absolutely nothing to do with you ever again. The thought of fucking you is revolting." It felt great to finally be able to tell her off. I had been dreaming of this moment since she'd left me. Well, after I got over the heartbreak of it. I was also a little bummed that Lauren wasn't here with me. I had told her about Tiffany after we started dating, and she was so pissed on my behalf that I knew if she was there she would have beat the ever-loving shit out of her. And I would've paid good money to see it.

Tiffany's expression was priceless. She looked as though I had slapped her across the face and then like she sucked on a lemon. Not used to being turned down, she huffed, rather unladylike I might add, and stomped off toward the exit without so much as another word for me. I smiled to myself as I made my way over to the weights.

As I lifted, my mind drifted to Lauren. I couldn't lose her. She was the one for me. I had already known that, but seeing Tiffany really cemented that all for me. For a long time I had thought that she was the woman I was supposed to be with, but now looking at her, I didn't see what I ever saw in that woman. Lauren was her complete and utter opposite in every sense of the word, for which I was very grateful.

I stared at myself in the mirror and mentally made myself a promise to do whatever I had to in order to get her back. She was the one for me and I wouldn't let her get away now. Not just when I had found her.

Chapter 26

Lauren

I had been back at Anna's for two weeks, and we were as close as ever. As far as my thoughts on Nix were concerned, I was still just as confused as when I left. It seemed that my mind wouldn't be made up with me spending time away from him. If anything it made things worse. My thoughts were playing over and over in my head, like a bad record on loop. I felt like I was going crazy.

Anna came home from work one day with Savannah in tow. Our friend had been crying and looked scared shitless.

"Savannah? What's wrong?" I asked.

"Greg's been released," she whispered.

"Charlie's working tonight so she's going to stay here with us," Anna said.

"Well, of course! We'll have a fun girls' night," I said, taking her hand and guiding her to the couch, trying to cheer her up a little bit so she didn't look so terrified.

"I'm so scared. What if he attacks me again? What if he actually kills me this time?"

"Savannah, do you know how to shoot a gun?" Anna asked calmly, to which Savannah shook her head. "I have an idea. Why don't the three of us take a class and get our concealed carry? Then we can get you a pretty pink gun and you can carry it with you everywhere you go. Would that make you feel better?"

Her eyes instantly lit up and some of the fear that had been coating her features vanished. "Yes! I would like to do that. Besides, it's not like I can be with someone every second of the day. That will make me feel so much better," she said.

"Okay then. I'll look into it and set us all up to take a class," I said, glad that Anna had thought of that. It would be a good thing for all of us to learn anyway.

After that, she visibly relaxed, but still seemed a bit tense. "Hey, do you guys want to do some yoga? I could lead a session for us. I think it would be good to get us all to relax," I said. Plus, we hadn't done yoga together in a long time; it would be a good bonding experience for us.

"Yes, bitch! Now you're thinking!" Anna yelled, excited now, as Savannah nodded in agreement.

We all changed into our yoga clothes and we went up into the studio. I positioned myself in front of the two girls so they could see me. Then, we lit a bunch of candles around the space so that it was a candlelit class, and burned some incense. Before we started, I also cleansed each of us with sage and then lit some palo santo to bring in positive energy, figuring we needed all the help we could get.

As we meditated beforehand, I thought of how I would guide us. I knew we needed some grounding, but I also thought that we should have some fire in there too, something to get our asses in gear. I led us in a mantra and then we got started. It began mostly on the floor, grounding, and then once we got warmed up I got us going in a vinyasa flow, before ending it on the floor once again. I made sure we had music with a good beat, to keep us moving. We closed with chanting ohm together.

When we were finished, I looked at the girls and realized all of us had tears in our eyes. That was when I knew it was a great session. We had moved and cleansed all of that shit we were hanging on to and left it on our mats. I got up and hugged the girls tightly. I had missed this, had missed them. We took a few deep, cleansing breaths together before I once again smudged us and the space with sage. I didn't want whatever we had gotten rid of to linger in the room.

After, I made each of them drink two glasses of water before we started in on the wine. None of us drank too much though, not wanting to get trashed after what we'd just accomplished. We turned on some music in the living room and sat around reminiscing and catching up. Instead of our normal Totino's pizza and brownies for dinner, we went healthy and made chicken, brussels sprouts, and kale.

"Mmm. This is delicious," Savannah said.

"Fuck yes it is," I agreed. "We should make this more often. Now we won't have food hangovers tomorrow."

We went to bed early that night, feeling sated in almost every way possible. Savannah slept in my bed with me since neither of us liked sleeping alone.

A week later, the three of us drove together to the class that I had found for us. It was taught by a retired cop, who had actually been SWAT toward his later years. We showed up ten minutes before it started and went inside. He greeted us and pointed to where we were supposed to be. He was nice, but had a very gruff way about him, pretty common for most men in that field.

It ended up being a class of all women, which I thought was fantastic. Not only did it make me feel more comfortable, but it was so brave of all of them to be doing this. We were taking our safety into our own hands.

"All right, ladies! Let's get started. The first thing we are going to learn is how to handle a weapon. So gather 'round. I'll show you here first, and then you'll go off to do it on your own," the instructor yelled.

We all watched as he showed us everything there was to know about a gun. How to load it, where the safety was and how to switch it on and off, how to hold it while you were loading it, how to check the chamber, all of it. He showed us twice and then sent us off to our own stations to do as he instructed. Anna was a natural, doing exactly as the instructor had done without pausing at all. It took me a moment to remember where the safety was, but I got the rest down after. Savannah looked nervous as all get-out to be handling a weapon, but did as she was told. She was a little shaky at first and had a hard time getting the clip with the bullets inserted, but after she practiced it a few times, she became a little more comfortable.

The instructor watched all of us carefully, giving us pointers when needed. When we all successfully loaded the gun, switched off the safety, checked the chamber, and unloaded the gun several times, we moved on to actually shooting the weapon. He showed us how to hold it, where to have your finger so you didn't accidentally discharge the weapon, and then finally how to shoot and how to expect the recoil to affect your body depending on what kind of gun you had. He also went into different strategies and techniques for firing to improve our marksmanship.

After he showed us all of that, he brought us over to the shooting range and lined us all up next to each other. As we all practiced, he walked behind us, observing and letting us get used to the weapons.

Once again, Anna was killing it. She had hit the target every time, only getting the outer edges a few times. The instructor came over and complimented her before continuing on.

"Have you done this before, Anna?" I asked.

"Bitch, please. Me?" she scoffed, effectively dismissing my question without answering it. I had a feeling she had, but didn't want us to know for some reason. Instead of pushing her, I let it drop, figuring she would tell me eventually if she wanted to.

We shot for about an hour, getting lots of practice in. I was actually pretty impressed with myself. While it had been a tad rough at first, by the end I was shooting the target every time and hitting the center with several shots. Savannah was improving by the end too. It seemed that she had just needed to get over her initial nerves and get into the groove.

The instructor then showed us how to properly care for and clean the guns. He also went over proper places to store them and safe ways to do it. The next part was fairly boring, but necessary, going over all of the state laws on owning firearms and the legal requirements.

In the end, we had to do a series of tests in order to get our concealed carry. They were fairly straightforward, especially considering we'd had so much practice time earlier in the day. Everyone passed the class, and we all left with big smiles on our faces.

"Hey, do you guys wanna go buy guns now? I'm kind of all pumped up to do this," I asked.

"Hell yes! I want my pretty pink gun!" Savannah exclaimed.

An hour later, we all had our weapons, all of them pink and black of course, and headed home feeling safe and proud of ourselves.

Chapter 27

Phoenix

One week later...

"Dude, what the fuck is up with you?" Charlie asked.

"Fuck off, man," I snapped.

"That's exactly what I mean. Nix, no one here at the station wants to even be around you anymore. You're being the biggest asshole lately. Is something going on with Lauren?"

"Don't pretend like you don't know. I'm sure Savannah has told you already."

"She hasn't told me anything, man. She's been too freaked out about Greg getting out of jail to gossip."

"Oh, shit. Greg is out?" I asked. That was not good.

"Yeah. He didn't have a previous record so he got out on good behavior. I know that fucker is going to make a move at some point, but all we can do right now is wait. Savannah's anxiety is through the roof."

"I bet. Well, if you guys need anything let me know," I offered.

"Will do. Thanks. Now, back to the subject at hand, what the hell happened?" he asked.

"Lauren found out about the accident. She got pissed and hurt and left."

"She was mad because you were in the ambulance with her?" he asked, confused. I hadn't told him about her hallucination. I filled him in, and his eyes got wider and wider as the story went on. "Oh, fuck" was all he said at the end of it.

"I know," I replied dejectedly.

"Well, you have to fix this."

"Dude, I know! I just don't know what to do. I even have something for her when she comes back. If she comes back."

"Just go to her. She told you she wanted space, but she probably just wants you. The longer you stay away, the harder it will be to get her back," he told me.

"You're right. Okay, I'll text her."

Hey, can I come to see you? I miss you, I typed, hoping like hell she would give me the time of day.

I still haven't made up my mind, Phoenix.

No pressure, I just want to see you. Please?

Okay. I'm off on Saturday. Three days away. Better than nothing.

I'll be there at noon.

I felt better having a time to meet up with her. I knew I had to get her back, I just hoped that she forgave me. She had to. I would spend the rest of my life making it up to her if I had to.

***

Saturday finally came. I woke up that morning both nervous and excited. Hopefully the conversation would go well and Lauren would be home with me by that night. I woke up at six, immediately wanting to go to her, but knowing I needed to wait, so I kept myself busy. I worked in the shop, finishing another piece to sell.

That was one thing that was going really well for me. I was making and selling tons of pieces on Etsy. Plus, it helped distract me while Lauren was gone. Being in the shop was all I wanted to do. So far I had sold around fifteen items, most of them priced at over a hundred dollars. I never would have even considered doing any of this if it hadn't been for Lauren, and I was very grateful. Maybe I would even make this my full-time business someday, I thought.

When I was finished, I took a shower, making sure to shave all my scruff off. I wanted to look nice and put together for her. I mentally rolled my eyes at myself; I sounded like a girl. Nevertheless, I put on some jeans and a nice shirt, styling my hair as well, something I rarely did. It was my own way of showing her that I was really willing to work for this and do whatever she needed me to.

When I was all ready to go, I headed out. On the way, I stopped to get her some flowers, knowing that was what most men did when they fucked up with their woman. I showed up to Anna's apartment at 11:58, not wanting to get here earlier than I told her. I got out of my car and started walking toward her door. Just when I was about to cross the street, a lady got out from her car and quickly ran over to me. She stopped a few feet in front of me. For the longest minute, she just stared at me. Her hair was disheveled and scraggly, and she was wearing really ratty clothes, like she hadn't changed or showered in the longest time. Her face was pale and her eyes were red and swollen.

"Can I help you, ma'am?" I asked.

"You've already done enough, Mr. Narrow," she said, her voice haunted. In that moment recognition hit, and I could tell this wasn't going to be good. It was the woman I saved from jumping off the building. Suddenly, she raised her arm and I was staring down the barrel of a gun.

I raised my arms up in surrender. "Miss, don't do this. You need help. I can get help for you." I tried reasoning with her, but it was hard to think of what to say with a gun pointed in my face. My breath started to come faster and my heart was pounding a dangerous rhythm in my chest.

"No one can help me, you bastard. They put me in psych for weeks because of you. I hate you so much. I hate you worse than I hate myself."

"Why do you hate yourself so much?" I asked, trying to keep her talking.

"None of your fucking business, asshole!" she screamed at me. She was swaying and I could smell liquor in the air.

"Have you been drinking, miss?" I asked gently.

"So what if I have?" she slurred.

"Well, you probably wouldn't be doing any of this if you were sober. If you leave now, I won't tell anyone what happened. Just leave."

"Liquor is the only thing that helps," she said softly.

"Helps with what? Do you have a drinking problem?"

"Yes," she said as her hand started shaking. "I've tried to get help for it many times, but it never works."

"Is that why you hate yourself so much?" I asked.

"It's what led to why I hate myself so much," she whispered, almost like she didn't want to say why out loud.

"What happened? You can tell me."

She looked at me hesitantly. For a moment it seemed like she was having a mental argument with herself. Finally, she cleared her throat and began, "One day, about two years ago, I was out of liquor, having finished my bottle, so I got in my car to head to the liquor store. I knew

I shouldn't be driving, but I needed more booze so I kept going. Before I knew it, I crashed into another car, T-boning them. The impact hadn't affected me much, but when I looked at the other car it was in pretty bad shape. The two people inside weren't moving. At the time, there was no one around and I was scared so I took off. I parked my ruined car in the garage and haven't touched it since. That night on the news I saw the story. I had killed a man. The woman was in the hospital. She had been pregnant. I'm sure that the accident caused her to lose her baby."

The further she got into her story, the more my stomach plummeted. It was Lauren. This woman was responsible for all the pain and suffering that she had gone through. And I had saved her. And now she was about to kill me. The universe couldn't be that cruel to Lauren, could it?

"If you've hated yourself for two years, why did you just recently try to commit suicide?" I asked.

"For a long time I tried to become a better person, thinking that if I could do that, then it would maybe make up for what I did. I quit drinking and tried to clean up my act. But after so long, I realized that nothing helped and that the guilt was eating away at me. I started drinking again, and at that point I knew I couldn't live anymore. A terrible person like me shouldn't be on this earth anymore. And neither should you. You kept me here when I shouldn't be. So I'm going to kill you, and then myself," she sneered, resolve hardening her features.

I closed my eyes, knowing there was nothing I could do as a shot was fired.

Chapter 28

Lauren

It was 11:50 and I was pacing the entire length of our apartment. I was so nervous to see Phoenix. Why wasn't he here yet? I knew he said noon, but he was usually early. I looked out the window to the front every twenty seconds, getting more and more anxious every time he wasn't there. Finally at 11:58 I saw his car pull up and I breathed a sigh of relief. He was carrying flowers with him, which was sweet.

All of a sudden, I saw a woman stop in front of him. I frowned, thinking that was odd. After they talked for a minute, she pulled a gun out and pointed it at his face. I didn't even think, I just got my gun and ran down the stairs. Luckily, she was facing away from the entryway to the apartment, so I was able to sneak down behind her. I lifted my own weapon, and had it pointed at her back. I was about to yell at her, when I heard her tell Phoenix all about the car accident she had caused. Halfway through the story, my heart sank and soared in the same moment. This was the woman. And here she stood in front of me, with a legitimate reason for me to shoot her. This was what I had been wanting since Ryan died. But as I stood there, I didn't feel hate like I thought I would. Instead, I felt sorry for her. Tears streamed down my face as I stood frozen behind her.

"So I'm going to kill you, and then myself," I heard her say. Without a second thought, I pulled the trigger. I wouldn't let her take another thing from me, no matter how sorry I felt for her. She fell to the ground, stunned, as the gun fell from her hands. She looked up at me, tears in her eyes, and said, "Thank you." With that, she passed out.

Phoenix's eyes, which had been closed when I pulled the trigger, popped open with the words that fell from her lips. He locked eyes with me for a split second, so many emotions flashing through them—relief, gratitude, regret, love. It felt as if in that one second, we had a whole conversation. We broke eye contact and I fell to my knees next to the woman, putting pressure on the wound on her upper back to slow the bleeding.

Nix immediately had his phone out and was calling 911. Within minutes, there were sirens blaring and cars screeching to a halt all around us. They wheeled the woman away on a gurney and the ambulance took off. The cops were next, taking both of our statements and going over every single detail with us.

What felt like years later, we walked up to the apartment. Luckily Anna had been at work all day, so she didn't witness any of the drama. We made our way to the bathroom, where I stripped off my bloody clothes, and threw them in the trash before turning the shower on. Phoenix followed suit, and soon we were both underneath the spray. The weight of what happened crashed into me hard, and I started sobbing. Phoenix pulled me into his arms and cradled me against his chest. We stood like that for ten minutes. When I finally settled, I pulled back to look him in the eyes.

"I thought I was going to lose you too," I said, new tears falling down my cheeks.

"You didn't let that happen, sweetness. Thank you so much. You saved my life," he said, moisture gathering in his eyes too.

"I couldn't let her take you from me. I love you, Phoenix."

"Oh, thank God. I love you too, Lauren. So much," he replied, kissing me deeply. "I'm so sorry for what happened with the accident. I just knew that when you were lucid again that everything would be different for you. I wanted to delay the pain I knew you would be in for as long as I possibly could. I know it was wrong and that I should have told you about it much sooner, but I just didn't want to hurt you any more than you already were. I only want the best things for you, sweetness. Can you ever forgive me?"

"I know, Phoenix. I've been so upset with you, but I understand why you did it. Just don't keep anything like that from me again, okay? Even if it hurts, we need to work through it together."

"I promise," he said, sealing it with a tender kiss. "Will you come back home now?" he asked.

"Yes, of course," I said, kissing him again. I had missed him so much.

We took our time with each other. Not making love, but teasing each other and enjoying our bodies. When we got out of the shower, we toweled each other off before getting dressed and heading into the kitchen. I poured us each a glass of wine, figuring after the experience we'd had that we would need to calm our nerves a bit.

"Are you hungry?" I asked.

"Famished. What do you have to cook? I can whip us up something," he said, looking through our fridge. We settled on stir fry, quick and easy. Twenty-five minutes later, we were scarfing down our dinner and finishing off our glasses of wine. We made sure to save enough food for Anna, figuring she would be hungry when she got off of work. When we were done, we went to my room to pack up my clothes once again so I could head back home with Phoenix. I was a little nervous to tell Anna, considering that he had been such a point of contention between us before, but I felt like things would be much better this time around. When we were about halfway done packing, Anna walked in.

"Hey, bitch! Ready to get our drink on?" she yelled upon entering the apartment.

Phoenix stayed behind as I joined her in the kitchen. I immediately poured a glass of wine and handed it to her as I took a drink from my own.

"Hey. So something happened today. Actually, let me rephrase. Lots of things happened today." I continued to tell her the whole crazy story. She was stunned. She yelled and exclaimed during multiple parts, looking utterly horrified, almost as much as I felt. As I was telling her, I realized that I was still in shock. I knew that the next day would be very rough for me, figuring it would take a minute to soak in. I concluded by telling her that Nix and I had made up. A twinge of jealousy crossed her features before I saw her visibly shove it down and put a happy look on her face.

"That's great, babe!" she said.

"You really think so?" I asked, still unsure of her reaction. I didn't want to create tension between us again when we had essentially just fixed things between us.

"Yes! Of course I do. I know I was a huge bitch before, but I've gotten past that, and I'm so happy that you guys have fixed things." She held up her wineglass in cheers to me. "Is he here?"

"Yes. He's in my room. He was giving us some time alone so I could tell you everything that had happened."

"Nix! Get your ass out here! And bring your wine!" she yelled loud enough for the whole apartment complex to hear.

He came out of my room smiling, holding his wineglass up to cheers as well. We told her that we had saved some dinner for her, and while she was eating, I told her that I would be heading home with Nix that night. She was a little sad, but mostly excited for us. When she finished eating, she came into my room to help us pack.

Even though I was sad to leave, I felt much better than the last time I left. This was what it should be like. Bittersweet. We spent the night packing, talking, and laughing, and I felt more content than I had in a while.

When we had all of my stuff loaded in my car, she gave me a huge hug, wrapping me tightly in her arms. I didn't recoil from people touching me anymore, and I sunk into her embrace.

"I'll miss you, cunt. Don't be a stranger," she said, her voice slightly teary.

"I'll miss you too. Let's plan a day together soon. I promise I'll show up this time," I joked.

"Sounds great. Keep me updated with everything that happens with that woman."

"Will do." I gave her one more hug before taking off.

Phoenix and I pulled up to the house, and I breathed a sigh of relief. I was home. It was a wonderful feeling. We started unloading my car and bringing everything into the house. We weren't going to unpack tonight, but I wanted to get my stuff out of my car so it wouldn't be stolen during the night. You never knew in Denver.

When I took the first bag of stuff into my yoga studio, I gasped out loud. I teared up as I looked around the room. My chair that I had picked out had finally arrived, and Nix had put it exactly where I told him I had wanted it. But the thing that had me crying was the breathtaking bookshelf that was sitting behind it. I went up to it and ran my fingers over the wood, delighting in the smell of the stain permeating off of it, the smell that I would now always associate with him. The wood was a dark walnut. The frame was just plain rectangular, but there was a section that cut through the middle of the bookcase, running diagonally from one corner to the other. You could put things on either side of the diagonal section, as well as in the diagonal section itself in the middle. It was absolutely beautiful, and I had never seen anything like it. He had also bought me a few books to start since I had yet to move my collection over, putting them in the diagonal section. I was still admiring his handiwork when he came in and wrapped me in a hug from behind.

"Do you like it?" he asked.

"What, my tears aren't giving you enough of an indication?" I asked like a smart-ass.

"Yes, but I want to hear you say it."

"I love it, Phoenix. Thank you so much," I said as I turned around to kiss him. I sagged against him, finally realizing how exhausted I was.

"Are you ready for bed, sweetness?"

"Yes. I feel like I'm dead on my feet right now."

"Me too," he said, grabbing my hand and leading me to the bedroom. We climbed into bed and I moaned upon crawling in. I loved this bed. It was so comfortable. "Don't make those noises right now. I haven't had you in far too long and it's been a rough and tiring day for us both. If you keep making them, I won't be able to help myself," he said as he ground his erection into my backside.

"What if I don't want you to stop?" I asked, waking up a little.

"Tomorrow, sweetness. I have something planned for us, and you will need your strength for it. Sleep now," he said gently, kissing me tenderly.

"Well, how can I after that?" I whined.

"Close your eyes, woman," he reprimanded, making me laugh.

I did as I was told, and was asleep within minutes.

I woke up the next morning surprisingly well rested considering the events of the previous day. I stretched contentedly, reaching for Phoenix only to find myself alone. I frowned until I smelled butter, garlic, and onions. I quickly brushed my teeth and put my hair up in a ponytail before going downstairs to find Phoenix behind the stove, a spatula in one hand and his coffee in the other.

"You look so sexy while you're cooking," I said, pressing myself up against his back.

"Oh yeah? You ain't seen nothin' yet, darlin'." I chuckled.

"What are you making?" I asked, pouring myself a cup of coffee.

"Eggs over easy with sautéed mushrooms, onions, garlic, and tomatoes," he replied.

Saliva pooled in my mouth at the smell and his words; I was famished. He also made us some garlic toast and we were soon eating. It was even better than it smelled, and I thought to myself that I was extremely lucky to have a man who was such a good cook.

When we were done, he looked at me with heated eyes.

"I want you downstairs. Now," he growled as he started cleaning up.

"Yes, sir," I replied breathlessly.

I wiped my mouth before standing and walking toward the basement stairs, heat already pooling between my legs. When I felt my feet sink into the soft carpet at the bottom, I took a moment to appreciate the space. I had missed being down here. Whenever I entered this place, I felt calm, like everything was right in the world. I didn't need to think, or make decisions, or act. I just needed to come down here and react to whatever kinky thing Phoenix did to me. It was freeing.

As soon as I entered, I started stripping, leaving my clothes in a trail as I walked toward the bench, where I assumed he would want me today. When I was naked, I sunk down into child's pose on the floor, aiming my backside toward where he would come in after cleaning up the kitchen. It was equally relaxing and erotic lying here like this. Child's pose was always my go-to pose to calm down, so my heart rate was used to slowing down, but the added thrill of having him come down to find me completely exposed like this, especially after so much time apart, had me almost panting with need. I could feel liquid drip from my seam onto the pristine carpet beneath me, and I felt so naughty.

An eternity later, I heard the door open and him descend the stairs. When he got to the bottom, the rug absorbed any sounds, so I wasn't sure if he had moved at all upon seeing me. I waited where I was, goosebumps appearing over my skin in anticipation. A moment later, I felt his warm hand caress my backside. I moaned loudly at the contact. His fingers whispered over my flesh before disappearing completely and then smacking hard on my right ass cheek, making me gasp in surprise and delight.

I then felt his breath whoosh across my neck as he said in my ear, "I don't want you here right now. Today, you're going to be hanging in the air for me. All to do what I please with. Get up."

I rose and met his eyes. While his expression was unyielding, his eyes were warm. His gaze broke from mine and rose to the ceiling where there were brackets and hoops, the ones that I had noticed my first time down here. The ones that he told me that I hadn't been ready for yet, but that I would be soon. I guess I was finally ready.

"Are you going to tell me what you're going to do to me?" I asked.

"Well, I have to. It's quite a process. I would love to keep you guessing, but I need your cooperation for it. I'm going to suspend you from the ceiling. In plastic wrap." At my exhale, he continued. "I want you all exposed and open for me, at the perfect height to do whatever I want with. How does that sound, sweetness?"

All I could do was nod my head as I bit down on my bottom lip. I had never heard of anything like this, but it sounded thrilling, and I couldn't wait. His fingers trailed down my body until they reached the juncture of my thighs. He dragged them through my seam before pulling them up to my mouth, painting my lips with my juices.

"I see you like the idea," he said smugly as I licked them clean. He bent to take a nipple in his hot mouth. He sucked hard and fast, making it stand at attention before switching to the other side. He went back and forth between the two for a couple minutes, leaving me an incoherent mess before pulling back. He left me for a moment as he went to the chest and brought back two suction cups with little fringes on the insides and wires coming from both. He attached them to my breasts. Once they were firmly in place, he pressed a button and they started vibrating, the nubs in the middle stimulating my nipples. He quickly pulled away and set a stool down underneath all the hooks and hoops. He then grabbed a huge roll of purple Saran Wrap, bigger than I had ever seen, and stood in front of me. "Arms up," he said. When I did as he asked, he had me hold an end as he wound the plastic around my body in a sort of slutty-looking dress. My tits were nearly falling out of the wrap, but it was wound so tight that they weren't moving. It also pressed the vibrators tighter against me, making them even more relentless. The "dress" stopped about halfway down my ass, giving me enough support, but also giving Phoenix complete access to me. When he was satisfied there was enough, he had me stand on the stool he'd set up. My heart was beating with both nerves and excitement.

He proceeded to wind me in an intricate web until I wasn't sure how he was ever going to get me out. Still, the process only made me wetter, being its own weird form of foreplay, not to mention the fact that he kept turning the breast vibrators on and off, slowly driving me insane.

He was touching me all over my body, but in a methodical way, binding my legs as well as my torso. He did keep my arms free, for which I was grateful. While I was excited about what we were doing, I think I would have panicked slightly if my arms were bound. There were however handles positioned in front of me that I could grab on to, which I assumed I would definitely need once we got down to it.

Fifteen minutes later, he was done. I was fully suspended in the air, supported only by the plastic surrounding my torso and another set of wrap under my shins to brace my legs. I felt free, almost like I could fly. I nearly held my arms out wide like I could, but then I met Nix's hungry gaze. He started circling my body, like a predator hunting its prey, even though I couldn't go anywhere. If I could, I might've had the urge to run.

When he was out of sight and firmly behind me, my heart started beating even faster. I felt the vibrators turn on full blast and I moaned. I felt something wet, his tongue most likely, trail from my ankle all the way up the inside of my leg. Just before he reached my center, he switched to the other leg, making the same trail on that side. Suddenly, I felt something else at my entrance. I couldn't tell what it was, until I heard him inhale deeply. It was his nose and he was sniffing me. Oh, God. I was equally embarrassed and turned on at the same time. I tried to close my legs, but I wasn't able to since they were immobile in the wrap.

"Fuck, Lauren. I missed your scent. You smell delicious," he growled before his mouth dove into my folds. I cried out loudly at the sudden onslaught of sensations. His arms came up to wrap around my torso, his hands ending up on my ass, spreading my cheeks to give him better access. A few times I felt his fingers brush against my asshole, and the teasing just made me crazier. He also switched up the setting on the vibrators so that they were coming on in bursts. When I was about to come he pulled back and spanked me, hard, four times, twice on each cheek. "You aren't coming yet," he said, his voice rough. I dangled on the edge for a minute, my nipples still being stimulated. When it subsided marginally, he praised me before going back in. "Good girl." This time though, his tongue swiped all the way from my clit to my asshole, which he teased and rimmed for several minutes. I was too far gone to feel any embarrassment about it, and the more attention he paid to it, the more I liked it.

His fingers finally came into play as he brushed my pussy lips. He gathered some of the moisture seeping from me before spreading it around my entire cunt. He used both hands as he pinched and pulled at my lips on both sides. It was a sensation I wasn't used to since it was typically a neglected part of that anatomy. He was stimulating me in every way possible and it was driving me insane. He suddenly pulled back and rummaged around in the trunk for a moment before returning. He spanked me some more with his palm, mostly on my ass but a few strikes to my clit as well. When he was finished with that, he pressed something cold and wet against my back entrance, I tensed briefly before relaxing and letting him in. "Good girl," he praised again. It was another butt plug. This one felt bigger than the last one.

"This one is pure glass, sweetness. I can see right up into this beautiful hole of yours," he said, spanking me again.

"Phoenix, please," I begged.

He gave me what I wanted and plunged his fingers into my pussy as his other hand pressed against the plug. I felt his tongue against my clit again, his teeth gently biting down every so often and I built fast. I didn't think I would be able to hold it back this time.

"Phoenix, can I come? Please."

"Yes, Lauren. Come all over my fingers," he growled against me, the vibrations of his voice sending me over the edge. I felt myself clench around him and the plug; the orgasm was never-ending.

Chapter 29

Phoenix

Lauren's orgasm went on and on. I could feel her spasming against my hand over and over. I couldn't wait until it was my dick she was clenching around. I pressed my palm to my erection, needing a bit of friction as I watched her. The view was fantastic. She was hanging and trussed up just for my viewing enjoyment and her pleasure. Her legs were spread wide, my face even with her most intimate parts, and she was drenched for me. Her entire lower half was coated with her juices, and it was the most glorious sight I had ever witnessed. She was made for me. She was panting from her orgasm and it made her breasts heave with every breath, her tits threatening to spill out of the wrap. She was a vision in purple plastic, and all mine.

When she was finished, I moved the stool behind her and positioned myself at her entrance. I turned the breast vibrators on full blast again as I plunged inside her. As soon as I was fully seated, I groaned animalistically. She felt like heaven wrapped around me. I grabbed her hips as I pulled out of her and yanked her back onto me. This wasn't going to be slow or gentle, probably like most couples would be when they got back together. This was raw and aggressive. It was all of our pent-up frustrations and anxieties from the past month being finally put to rest. This was us at our most primal form.

I kept up the relentless pace, crashing into her again and again. Our lovemaking was loud as fuck, and I was sure the neighbors could hear, but I didn't give a shit. Lauren was the only thing on my mind. The world could have come to an end outside and I wouldn't have even known. I pushed my thumb against the plug still firmly in her ass, making her scream. I took out a vibrator from my back pocket and pressed it against her clit with my other hand.

Within moments, she was coming again, contracting around my cock in violent bursts. I almost came with her, but I wasn't ready for that yet. I slowed as I let her come down, and myself settle a bit. When I was confident I could last a bit longer, I started moving again as I grasped the plug. I gently started pulling it out and pushing it back in, moving it opposite to my thrusts into her pussy.

"Oh, God. Phoenix. I want you in my ass. Please, fuck me there. I need you," she begged me. Oh, fuck. This, I was not expecting or planning for.

"Are you sure, Lauren? Have you ever done that before?"

"I've never done it before. I want you to take my virgin ass. Now." I growled at her words. I pulled the plug out before going back to the chest to get more lube and a dildo, one that had a vibrator attached to the outer part for her clit. I turned it on and got it positioned deep inside her pussy. At her moan, I pulled it in and out a few times to tease her with it before leaving it there.

I applied a generous amount of lube to my cock before slathering a ton all over her backside. You could never use enough when it came to anal sex. I brought my cock to her crack, sliding between her cheeks for a few strokes before notching myself against her tight virgin hole. I slowly started pushing forward. She was accepting me fairly easily since she'd had a huge plug in her ass until a few moments ago, but I still took my time. Every glorious inch forward was strangling me. I had thought her pussy was tight, but it was nothing compared to this.

When I was fully inside, I stopped and held myself still, letting her adjust to me. "How're you doing, baby?" I asked.

"I just need another second," she whispered. I reached underneath to grasp the toy still buzzing inside her. I moved it in and out a few times, reawakening her pleasure and masking any discomfort she might be feeling. Soon she was moaning again, louder than before. "Move, Phoenix. Please move."

It was all the permission I needed. I pulled back and rocked in and out slowly, still being gentle with her, but she was soon telling me to fuck her harder and faster. I felt my orgasm closing in, not accustomed to the extreme tightness of her body.

"Phoenix, I'm going to come again. Come with me." Her breathy voice sent me over the edge as I spilled myself deep in her ass. I felt her follow me seconds later.

I pulled out of her and leaned down to press a kiss against her ass cheek. I quickly grabbed a warm, wet rag to wipe her down before we tackled the task of freeing her from the plastic.

I got out the scissors and cut the binds on her legs first before moving to her torso. When I got about a third of the way in, I positioned myself underneath her so I could support her weight once the wrap was no longer holding her. We were both chuckling as I worked, and soon she was free. I turned off the breast vibrators and removed them before handing her a plush pink robe that I kept down here just for her. She gratefully put it on before leaning in for a hug. We stood there, just holding each other for the longest time.

"I missed you so much," she told me.

"I missed you more, sweetness."

Chapter 29

We spent the rest of the week in domestic bliss. We were in a major honeymoon phase, and I couldn't remember ever having this much sex in my entire life. We got back into our routine, and it felt so right.

The cops had called us the day after the incident to let us know what happened. The woman who confronted me, whose name was Shauna White, had been taken to the hospital. When Lauren had shot her, the bullet had grazed her aorta. She was rushed into surgery but the doctors weren't able to save her. Lauren and I both felt bad for what happened, but were relieved that she didn't end up pulling through. We both knew that Shauna wouldn't have been happy and would have likely been put in a mental facility, a danger to society.

While it had been traumatic, I think it had given Lauren the closure she needed from the accident. I knew she had always wondered what happened to the driver, and now she had answers.

As for me, I had decided that I no longer wanted to be a firefighter. I had taken the plunge and put in my notice with the department. I was done risking my life. It had been fine when I didn't have someone special, but now that I had Lauren, I didn't want to do anything to endanger myself and possibly leave her alone again. Not that I worried if she would be okay, because I knew she would, she was so strong, but I didn't want to put her through that if I could help it in any way. This incident just cemented that for me and gave me the courage to do something different.

I dedicated my time to woodworking now, making it my full-time business, and I was happy to say that it was doing better than ever. It was fantastic to be able to do something that I loved for work as opposed to something I felt like I had to do.

Lauren was still at the hair salon, but she was teaching more classes, and had been able to start charging for them since she wasn't fresh out of school anymore, and she was building up quite a following. She was even thinking about starting her own YouTube page to see if she could make some money there as well. I knew people would love her immediately upon taking her first class, so I was positive she would be successful.

A month after she moved back in, Lauren asked me something. "Can we get a dog? I've always wanted one."

"A dog? You've never had one before?" I asked, stunned.

"No. I wanted one when I was a kid, but my mom would never let us have one. She always said, 'You can have as many dogs as you want when I'm dead.' And then when I lived with Ryan, he was allergic so we couldn't. Now that I'm settled in this house with you, it's something that I really want and that I feel ready for."

"Of course we can get one, sweetness. Do you have an idea of what breed you want?" I asked.

"No. Something medium-sized though, I think. I want to rescue one. So maybe we can go to the Humane Society and when we meet the right one we'll just know," she said hopefully.

"Do you want to go today?"

"Oh, can we?" she asked, bouncing up and down like a little girl.

"Of course. Let's get ready and do a once-over around the house to make sure it's safe for a dog, and then we can head over before we go to the pet store to get everything we'll need."

An hour later, we were sitting in the car in front of the Humane Society. Lauren was fidgeting in her seat, and I could tell she was nervous. I grabbed her hand and gave it a tight squeeze before getting out of the car, with her following suit. We walked in and told them we'd like to look at the dogs, and soon we were walking down aisles of cages, looking for our little fur mate.

We saw so many cute dogs, but none of them felt right. By the last aisle, I could tell Lauren was feeling dejected.

"Our dog is out there, sweetness, we just need to find them. Don't worry. If we don't find them here, we can look somewhere else," I told her, and she smiled at me.

All of a sudden, she stopped and turned at the sound of a whine. In the second to last cage, there was a pit bull and German shepherd mix. It wasn't a puppy, it looked to be at least two, and it was tan. It was lying down and had its head resting on its paws. It was looking up at Lauren like she was its new mommy and it really wanted her to take it home. She knelt down next to the cage and held her hand out for the dog to sniff. It did immediately before giving her a quick kiss on the hand. This was the one; I could see it written all over Lauren's face.

The lady showing us around noticed too and chimed in. "We've had this boy for about six months now. We aren't positive, but we think he's around two to three years old. We got a call about him being on the streets and extremely hungry. Some lady had found him and tried to get him but he was extremely skittish at that point, so she built him a shelter and left him some food before she called us. When we finally got him here he was extremely malnourished. He's finally healthy and getting more comfortable around people. I'm guessing that's why it's taken so long for him to get adopted." With every word, Lauren seemed to tear up a little more.

She cleared her throat before asking, "Can we meet him?"

"Of course," she said before taking her keys out to open his cage. I decided to hang back for a minute and let him meet Lauren first. Since he had been skittish when they got him, I didn't want to overwhelm him with too many people at once.

When his cage was open, he didn't come out immediately. Instead, he stood there for a minute, looking skeptical about meeting someone new, but also tempted. Lauren kneeled down and held out her hand to him, letting him come to her when he was ready. "Come here, baby. I won't hurt you," she cooed. Slowly, he inched out of the cage and sniffed her hand again before coming closer to her. When she was confident she could pet him, she did, and they were instantly in love. He licked her multiple times before snuggling up to her.

"Phoenix, come down and meet him. He's the sweetest baby ever."

I slowly walked up, making sure to take my time. Once I got close enough, I knelt down too so he wouldn't be as intimidated. I held my hand out to him and he looked at me skeptically, unmoving.

"It's okay, baby. This is Phoenix. He will take good care of you," Lauren said as she grabbed my outstretched hand. She held both of our hands down for him to sniff, and he finally did. I let him sniff me for as long as he needed. Finally, he graced my hand with a tiny lick.

"Good boy," I praised as I attempted to pet him. He let me, and soon the three of us were all sitting on the floor getting to know each other. Needless to say, we were smitten.

"We would like to adopt him," I told the lady showing us around.

"I figured," she said, smiling. "I'll go get the paperwork started."

An hour later, we had our little guy in the back seat of the car, and were heading to the pet store. We got everything we needed for him: food, a crate, treats, toys, a bed, food and water dishes, and a leash and a collar.

"You know, we still need to name him," Lauren pointed out as we headed home.

"How about Max?" I asked.

"Too plain. Buddha?"

"No. Bruce?"

"Eh. Bubba?" she asked.

"Maybe. What about Rex?"

"I like that, but it still feels too plain. I think it needs something in front of it. Ooh like Atticus! Atticus Rex!" she exclaimed and the dog barked from the back seat.

"Atticus Rex it is. And I see he likes it too."

"Do you like your new name, Atticus Rex?" she cooed at him from the front seat. When he barked again at her, as if replying, she petted him on the head and told him "Good boy."

We got home and unloaded everything. We put his crate in the living room downstairs, not wanting it in our room, his dog bed at the foot of ours, and all of his food in the kitchen. It took us a couple weeks to get to know each other, and for him to get acclimated to the house, but he ended up being perfect for us. Lauren loved having him with us. He originally was supposed to only sleep in his dog bed, but of course, after two nights Lauren wanted him in our bed. He slept there every night after.

The only other thing that I wanted was something that was crazy and that I knew was too soon. But one morning, I had just woken up from a dream where what I wanted had come true, and Lauren was stirring next to me. I cuddled up against her from behind, and realized that I wanted to wake up like this every single morning for the rest of my life.

"Marry me," I blurted. As soon as it popped out of my mouth, I mentally slapped myself. *You idiot.* What a way to propose. No ring. Nothing romantic or planned. But still, I awaited her answer.

She turned tired eyes to me, frowning in confusion. "Did you just say what I think you did?"

"Yes." While I hadn't meant to blurt it out, I meant it with everything in me.

"Of course I'll marry you."

"Really?" I asked.

"Why wouldn't I, Phoenix?" she asked, laughing.

"Well, I don't know. We haven't been together that long, I suck at proposals, I don't have a ring. Take your pick."

"I pick you. Every time. If this life has taught me anything, it's that everything can be taken from you in a single moment, so enjoy what you have when you have it. I love you so much and I would be honored to be your wife," she replied. Leave it up to her to sound like she was the one proposing.

"Is today too soon for you?"

Chapter 30

Lauren

We quickly got out of bed and showered together. There was so much to do and so little time! Phoenix tried to feel me up while we were in there but I batted his hand away. I needed to get ready and make myself all pretty if we were going to get married that day. I made a mental list of everything I needed to get done. I had to shave every inch of my body, as well as do my hair and makeup. And while we weren't having an actual wedding, I still wanted to be in a wedding dress, which meant that I would need to buy one before going to the courthouse. Oh God. The pressure. It was intense, but it was also so exciting.

Phoenix shaved his face clean as well, but was still out of the shower way before me. Shit, I also needed wedding night lingerie. I would have to make a stop by Fascinations after I got my wedding dress. Oh, and we didn't have rings. There was so much to do!

"Phoenix!" I yelled for him as I was shaving my legs.

"What's wrong?" he asked as he entered the bathroom.

"We don't have rings! And I'm not doing something cheesy like wrapping yarn around our fingers until we find something."

"I can go get them for us while you finish up here," he said calmly.

"Well, I need to get a wedding dress too. Do you have a suit that you can wear?"

"Oh, you want to dress up? I thought we would just go and do it," he said nonchalantly.

I stopped what I was doing, which was saying something considering I was in such a hurry, and looked at him like he'd grown two heads. "Are you fucking kidding me?" I asked. While I was totally fine not having a traditional wedding—I actually preferred it since I had been planning a wedding with Ryan and knew what a pain in the ass it was—I still wanted to look beautiful on my wedding day.

He held up his hands in surrender as he said, "Never mind. Forget I said that. I have a suit I can wear. I'll get the rings and meet you at City Hall?" he asked as I breathed a sigh of relief. I gave him a quick nod as I went back to shaving. He popped his head in the shower to give me a quick but passionate kiss. "See you soon, almost wifey," he whispered, making me smile and swoon. It helped calm me down marginally. By the end of the day we would be married.

"Don't get me an engagement ring. I don't need one. Just a simple-ish wedding band. Rose gold, please. I'm a size six," I told him.

"Got it. I love you."

"I love you," I replied, holding his gaze.

He took off and I finished showering and shaving. Luckily, I had just gotten my eyebrows and upper lip waxed and my nails done a few days prior, so I didn't need to worry about any of that. Little A-Rex could feel my nervous, excited energy and was following me around closely, probably assuming something was wrong. I patted him on the head and told him he was a good boy and that everything was fine before going back to getting ready.

I quickly round-brushed my hair. I wasn't sure what else to do with it at the moment, because I didn't know what kind of dress I would end up getting. In the end, I curled it and put a shit ton of bobby pins in my purse figuring that I could fuck with it before the wedding, once I had a better idea of what I was working with. For makeup, I went with a simple but dramatic smokey eye that included some blush pink. I went a little crazy highlighting my cheekbones, but figured fuck it, it was my wedding day. I smiled broadly at the thought. I did my lips up with a cool dusty rose color in a matte finish. Satisfied with my face and hair for the moment, I packed up all my makeup and hair stuff that I thought I might need, as well as almost every piece of jewelry I owned, once again figuring I would see what worked once I had my dress.

Luckily, it wasn't the weekend, so David's Bridal was absolutely dead. As soon as I walked in they took me straight back. I told them I was getting married as soon as I found a dress, and they brought me a ton of options, helping me to get in and out of the store as quickly as I could.

They had me try on some tea-length dresses, but those didn't really feel like me, even though I was getting married at City Hall. I didn't want a train, but I did want a floor-length dress. Once I figured that out, it went a little faster. There was a strapless one that I liked, but it was too formal and tight. I wanted something fun and carefree, maybe slightly hippie-ish. I wanted lots of lace, and I didn't want white. I wanted at least ivory or champagne. I told them all of this, and in the end we found the perfect dress.

It was ivory, and almost all lace. It had long sleeves, and the neckline came all the way up to my throat, but the best part was the back. It was backless, cutting into a deep V that ended just above my ass. I felt beautiful and free-spirited. Suddenly, all my worries about the rest of the day fell away. This was what I had been anxious about, finding a dress in such a short amount of time that I actually wanted to wear.

Next was shoes, which they luckily had at the store. I found a pair that matched my dress perfectly. They were flats, ivory and lace with a rounded toe. Nothing over the top, just perfect.

I was in and out in an hour. Not bad, I thought. My next stop was to Fascinations, and I went straight to the bridal section.

The wedding lingerie was all cute, but they were all too white. Just when I was about to say fuck it and leave, I saw it in the regular lingerie section. It was an ivory corset with straps, but the lace running down the middle of it had bits of light pink in it, the exact shade of my hair. I picked my size off the rack, not even bothering to try it on, as well as some stockings with lace at the top to match the corset, and some white lace panties to complete the look. I would put the panties on with the dress, but the rest would have to wait until we were at home.

My last stop was to Sprouts right next store. I wanted a bouquet. I ran to the flower section and glanced around. There were some beautiful flowers in season. I just needed to pick one and go.

"Can I help you, miss?" a nice lady behind the counter asked.

"Well, I'm getting married as soon as I leave here, I just need to pick a bouquet." Surprise, then delight flashed over her features.

"Oh, how fun! Okay, well, for wedding flowers, I always love peonies. We of course also have roses if you want to go the more traditional route. Oh, and we also just got in these dahlias. We have a bouquet with red, orange, and pink."

"Yes! Let's do the dahlias, please."

She picked up one of the bouquets, trimmed the ends off, and wrapped it in ribbon before sending me on my way. I drove like a bat outta hell to get to City Hall. I checked my phone to see that Phoenix was already there and getting everything set up. I texted him that I needed to get ready and I would be there soon.

I headed into the ladies' room with all of my stuff. I threw on my dress, which luckily didn't have any zippers or anything complicated, along with the bridal panties (sans bra because my dress was backless) and the shoes. When I came out of the stall, there was a group of ladies gathered around the sink, chatting.

Upon seeing me, they all gasped and exclaimed, "Oh my God!"

"Are you getting married?" one asked, to which I almost rolled my eyes, because honestly, what else would I be doing in a wedding dress at City Hall?

"Of course she is, you idiot. You look beautiful!" another one said, making me laugh.

"Thank you," I replied.

"Do you need help with anything?"

I was about to tell them no, but then I looked at my hair. I was in a bit of a rush. "Actually yes, would you ladies mind?" I asked.

"Not at all! What do you need?"

"Can you pin these curls in the back? I need to do a braid in the front and I'm in a bit of a hurry." They did as I asked and started pinning the curls in a section to make it almost look like a messy bun to the side. While they were working, I started a Dutch braid with my bangs that swept off to the side. It was going to be huge and beautiful. Once I was finished with that, I touched up my makeup and chose some long dangly rose-gold earrings with feathers and leaves, as well as a matching bracelet. The girls finished just as I put on my jewelry.

I stared at myself in the mirror and couldn't believe what I saw. I couldn't believe this was happening to me. Finally. The girls exclaimed and did all the things women do when they see someone else in a wedding dress. I thanked them and they left me alone. When they were gone, I took out the necklace still around my neck that held my engagement ring from Ryan.

"Ryan, I'm sorry you aren't here, but thank you for everything" was all I said as I kissed the ring and put it back in place, under my dress. While I missed Ryan, I knew I was meant to be with Phoenix. And none of this would've happened if he was still here. I no longer felt conflicted. Just sure.

I took a deep breath and left the bathroom. I put everything in my car before meeting Phoenix at the location he had texted me. Upon seeing me, he gasped, his eyes roaming over every inch of me before meeting and holding my gaze. So many words were spoken in that one glance. I, in turn, took my fill of him. He looked delicious. His hair was slicked back in his "fancy" hairstyle, and his face was clean-shaven, something I rarely got to see 'cause he almost always had scruff. He was wearing a charcoal gray suit with a button-up white shirt and the burgundy tie he wore to Savannah and Charlie's wedding.

"Lauren, you look breathtaking. I've never seen a more beautiful bride," he whispered to me. I smiled as I turned in a circle, letting him see the back of my dress. He groaned low in his throat and I felt his fingers caress the flesh that was exposed. "Let's get married so I can get you home and take this gorgeous dress off of you," he murmured in my ear so no one else could hear.

"I got something else to wear for you when we get home," I said, making him groan again.

"Phoenix and Lauren?" a judge called when he came out into the hallway. We raised our hands and followed him into his chambers. "Do you have vows?" he asked. We shook our heads. We hadn't had time for that. He nodded as he grasped a sheet off of his desk. He read the typical wedding vows out loud as we each said "I do." It all was fairly quick and nothing like a normal ceremony. You could tell he did this multiple times a day, but I didn't care. I was marrying Phoenix and that was all that mattered.

When it came time to exchange rings, Phoenix pulled them both out of his pocket and put mine on first. I gasped upon seeing it. It was rose gold just like I asked, but the skinny band had black diamonds all across one side. He slid it on my finger and it felt and looked perfect sitting there. He kissed my finger after it was on and then it was my turn. He handed me his band and it was very fitting, and matched mine in color. It was an all-black band except for the strip of rose gold that cut through the middle. I smiled as I slipped it on his hand.

"I now pronounce you husband and wife. You may now kiss the bride," the judge said. We leaned in and he gave me a short but passionate kiss. When we broke apart, the judge said, "Just sign here." We signed and that was it.

We walked outside and Phoenix picked me up off my feet and twirled me around in his arms. I laughed loudly, happier than I'd ever been before. He kissed me again, this time it lasted longer since we didn't have an audience. Until I heard a group of women exclaiming.

"Oh my God, there they are! Look at how cuuuuute!" I immediately recognized the voice from the bathroom.

"Is this your husband?" the other asked.

Phoenix and I broke apart so we could address them. "Yes, this is my husband, as of ten minutes ago," I said, giggling.

"Have you guys gotten any pictures taken yet?" My face fell at the question. Shit! I had forgotten about that. We wouldn't have any pictures of the wedding! "I can see by your face, you haven't. It's okay! We can take some of you now. Just give me your phone and we can take a bunch of you both." These girls were turning out to be my saving grace. I handed her my phone, and what originally started out as her taking a few pictures, quickly turned into a full-blown photo shoot with her telling us how to pose and where to stand. We had so much fun and were laughing the whole time.

We got home an hour later, and I changed into my bridal lingerie as Phoenix let out our little hellion. When he came back upstairs, I was lying across the bed, waiting for him. He stood there just staring at me for a solid ten seconds before he growled and attacked. That night, he made love to me for hours as we basked in our newly married glow.

The next day, I woke up feeling incredible. I had almost forgotten what happened the day before until I woke up fully. When it all came flooding back, I squealed in excitement. Nix's eyes popped open at the noise.

"What? What's wrong?" he asked, concerned.

"Nothing is wrong. Everything is right," I said, snuggling up to him, "husband."

We cuddled in bed all morning and had the perfect lazy day.

"Shit. We haven't told anyone yet. I should go let Anna know. She will be pissed if I don't. And we need to tell Charlie and Savannah too," I said.

"Well, do you want to have them over for dinner this week?"

"Yes, but I need to go tell Anna."

"Okay, sweetness. Get dressed and go tell her. I'll work in the woodshop for a little bit," he said easily, kissing me before swatting me on the ass.

I quickly got ready and texted her to make sure she was at home. When she replied that she was, I told her that I was coming over because I had something important to tell her. She replied that she did too and that she would see me soon.

I walked into the apartment fifteen minutes later. "Anna! I'm here!" I yelled. I was slightly nervous that she was going to freak out on me again, but I pushed past it.

"In the studio!" she yelled back.

I went upstairs to find her smudging the space. I breathed in deeply, letting the smell of sage comfort and calm me.

"Hey," I said. She turned around to look at me and I saw anxiety prominent in her features, and her hand was shaking slightly. "Is everything okay?" I asked as I went over to hug her.

"Yes and no. Everything is fine, but I'm a bit of a mess. There's something I think I need to tell you. Something that I've been debating saying to you, but I think I need to," she rambled as she stared into my eyes.

"You can tell me anything, Anna. You know that."

She continued to stare at me before she suddenly wrapped her hand around my neck, pulling me forward before she pressed her lips to mine in a gentle kiss. I was so stunned that I just stood there.

"I'm in love with you, Lauren."

Author Notes

Want more? Anna's story is next in *The Fire Inside Me*.

Sign up for my newsletter for all the latest information on my upcoming books!

http://eepurl.com/hRZzz5

Thank you all so much for reading, and I hope that you enjoyed Lauren's story! If this is the first book you've read of mine, make sure to go back and read Savannah and Charlie's story, *Fire & Ink*.

If you enjoyed this novel, please leave me a review! I appreciate all of you!

I love hearing from my readers! Find me on...

Instagram: @L.J.Burkhart.author
Pinterest: @LJBurkhartbooks
Email: LJBurkhartbooks@gmail.com

Acknowledgments

You know? Everyone said that writing my second novel would be much harder than writing my first. I would like to say, for the record, that I think they were full of shit. This one was much easier for me, but I have a ton of people to thank. As they say, it takes a village.

To my husband, you have been a huge help to me during this process. From little things, like keeping me company while I write, to helping me during this crazy publishing process. I am so grateful for you.

To my mother and sister, you ladies are always there to give me your opinion on my writing, and I value your input so much. I love you both and am so thankful to have your brilliant minds showing me avenues to go down that I never would have even thought of. Thank you for always believing in me and supporting me.

To Iris, words cannot express how much you have contributed to this book and how much I appreciate all of your input. This would not be the same novel without all of your brainstorming sessions and ideas.

To my aunt Amy, your high school English teacher advice has come in so handy throughout this whole process, and I feel honored that you make time to read my novels even though you are so busy. I hope you enjoyed this one as much as the first.

To Rebecca, thanks for being one of my cheerleaders and guinea pigs during this hectic time in your life. I appreciate you.

To Sheba, my sweet doggie, thanks for always keeping my company while I write, and not bothering me too much when I'm on a roll.

To my editor, Beth, thank you so much for all of your hard work on my novels. It has been so fun working with you. I really appreciate all of your time and patience, and I really enjoy reading all of your comments you leave me.

To my graphic designer, Les, thank you for another beautiful cover. You knocked it out of the park again.

And finally, to you, dear reader, thank you so much for taking this journey with me. I hope you have enjoyed reading my novels as much as I've enjoyed writing them! I appreciate all of your continued support.

About the Author

L.J. Burkhart is the author of the new novel *Fire & Ink*. She writes contemporary romance and may eventually venture into fantasy. Her latest works are the sequels in the *Fire & Ink* trilogy, *Light Me Up* and *The Fire Inside Me*. L.J. has been a lifelong writer, starting with songs and poetry in the third grade, before eventually moving on to novels in her early twenties. When she isn't coming up with dramatic plot twists and steamy sex scenes, you can find her doing yoga, hanging out with her best bitches, baking, or reading, curled up on the couch with her husband and dog with a big glass of red wine.

You can connect with me on:

- 🌐 https://ljburkhart.wixsite.com/ljburkhartbooks
- 🔗 https://www.instagram.com/l.j.burkhart.author
- 🔗 https://www.pinterest.com/ljburkhartbooks

Subscribe to my newsletter:

- ✉ http://eepurl.com/hRZzz5

Made in the USA
Middletown, DE
06 November 2023

41955236R00123